KAYLA WREN

# Her Mountain Rescue

BLACK CHERRY
PUBLISHING

# Contents

# Keep in touch with Kayla!

Want to hear about new releases, sales, bonus content and other cool stuff? Sign up for Kayla's newsletter at www.kaylawrenauthor.com/newsletter!

# 1

# Bianca

*Eighteen months ago*

The cookout is a sea of flannel and worn denim; baseball caps and faded corduroy. Bursts of laughter echo above the chatter of the crowd, and a group of kids toss a ball back and forth by the lake's edge. The late afternoon sun is burnished gold, the breeze tickling dried red leaves where they cling to tree branches. Meat hisses and spits on the huge outdoor grill.

The end of summer is here. Finally.

I lower a crate of glass soda bottles onto a picnic bench, nudging a pile of napkins out of the way with one corner. Every single picnic table is piled high with food and drink, the old wood groaning under their weight, but the crowd is relentless. Hands snake out, grabbing a paper plate here, a soda bottle or cold beer there, and the food and drink disappears as fast as the volunteers can replace it.

It's a Mountain Rescue cookout. These are some hungry, hungry people.

I grab a beer before slipping through a gap in the crowd, smiling and nodding at the faces I recognize. It's a mixed crowd: half locals like me, who grew up here and never felt pulled to leave, and half new residents, drawn here by the mountain peaks or the quiet town life. I'm glad they're here—new blood in the town is always a good thing—but the press of strangers is kind of overwhelming. I duck and weave my way to the edge of the crowd, spilling out into the cool breeze and sipping gratefully at my beer.

Jeez. You'd think I'd be used to this by now. The kids are a million times worse at the end of summer camp party.

The lime wedged down the neck of the bottle gives the beer a nice kick, and I hum as I shade my eyes and scan the crowd. I'm looking for dark hair, sparkling green eyes and a curved, sensual mouth; a wicked laugh and sculpted shoulders. I've picked Ezra out of crowds plenty of times in the six months we've been dating. He's so much larger than life, so magnetic, that he's impossible to miss, but it's not him my eyes snag on this time.

Warm brown eyes. A slight frown creasing a broad forehead. Short tawny hair and a matching beard. Those strange eyes bore into mine, their frown deepening, and I'm pinned to the spot. Can't look away. As he holds my gaze, heat spreads through my body, creeping through my limbs like the sun sliding over the mountain peaks.

My palm grows clammy against the glass beer bottle. I hear my own breaths louder than the crowd.

"Bee!"

I jolt as a hand claps onto my shoulder, squeezing gently. Ezra beams down at me, his face so open and bright, and I force a smile in return.

2

"Hey. Um, you're here." The noise of the crowd rushes back in. Beneath my thin navy shirt, my heart pounds a mile a minute.

Who *was* that guy?

Ezra's smile fades slightly. "Yeah. Yeah, of course I'm here. You weren't waiting, were you?"

"No." It's true. I arrived less than ten minutes ago. And yet somehow, in that time, I've managed to stare at another man then make *Ezra* feel bad. Guilt pinches my stomach, and I grab a handful of his t-shirt. It's soft from hundreds of washes, red cotton with a long-faded logo. The hard planes of Ezra's chest brush against my knuckles, and I swallow hard. "No, I wasn't waiting. But I *am* glad to see you."

"Good." A cocky smile stretches over his face. And yeah—I see it. Why Ezra has such rabid fans, his following online bigger than the population of this whole town. The man is a force of nature. A star without trying. "Maybe later you can see as much of me as you want."

"I'll hold you to that," I murmur as he places a broad hand on my back and steers me further towards the lakeside. For as much as Ezra likes to joke around, he's always keeping an eye out for me. He knows I don't do well in big crowds—of adults, anyway. And though he puts on this big showman persona, he's considerate to a fault.

"I know what you're doing." My sneakers scuff over the dried September grass. It's unseasonably hot today, the final gasp of a long, hot summer before the harsh Lonely Mountain winter reminds us all who's boss. "You're managing me again."

Ezra stops beside the sparkling water, expression pained. "It's not *managing*. I'm looking out for you."

"I'm a grown woman. You don't need to—"

Ezra raises an arm, waving and grinning over the top of my

head. I hide a smile, rolling my eyes before turning to meet the newcomer.

I stop cold, heart pounding again.

"Bee, this is Caleb Olsen. He's my new partner in the Mountain Rescue team."

"Hi," I manage.

"Hello."

The man's voice is deep. Steady. It suits him, from his towering height to his barrel chest. Caleb looks less like a man and more like a feature of the landscape, and it's no wonder he caught my eye in the crowd. Even Ezra looks a little dazed as he grins at his partner.

Caleb watches me closely. "Are you enjoying the cookout?"

I open my mouth to answer, but Ezra beats me to it.

"Bianca? Hell no. She hates crowds, don't you, Bee?"

I shrug one shoulder, still trapped in Caleb's gaze. "I like the lake, though. And the beer."

His mouth quirks up at the corner.

Ezra looks between us, bouncing on his heels. He's happy, caught up in the crackling energy of the cookout, and my throat is tight as I force my gaze back to my boyfriend.

It's no hardship. Magnetic Caleb or no, Ezra is the most beautiful man I've ever seen.

"Caleb and I are on shift later." Ezra raises his soda to illustrate his point, and I glance at the bottled water in Caleb's hand. "Gotta save the tourists from themselves. Right, man?"

"Right."

"Dream team," I murmur stupidly, then my cheeks flame bright red, as though I've said something dirty rather than inane. And that is *not* what I meant, but now I've heard my own words, I can't un-think it.

4

Ezra. Caleb. Ezra *and* Caleb.

Oh, god. I've got a one-way ticket to hell.

If Ezra notices my blush, he doesn't mention it. He's too busy pulling out his phone, showing Caleb the route he climbed this morning. He zooms in on gear placement, and even though there's no way a big man like Caleb climbs, he hums and makes all the right noises. Points out the state of the rock face; asks about weather conditions.

But now and then, his brown eyes flick to me. To the blush still staining my cheeks.

"You know what?" I push my hair back from my forehead. "I actually have a headache. I might take off and lie down at home."

"You want company?" Ezra frowns at me, concern creasing his perfect features. He shoves his phone back in his pocket. "I could take care of you. Bring you iced water; pop you some pills."

God, I'm the worst.

"Nope." My sneakers kick through the grass as I back up a step, the blades whispering against my faded jeans. Then another. "You guys just got here! And you're working later, so. Have fun."

"Are you sure?" Ezra calls as I wheel around, throwing a thumbs up over my shoulder as I plunge back into the crowd. I'm being rude, acting so weird, but I'll make it up to him tomorrow. Tell him my headache got the better of me. My phone buzzes in my pocket, but I ignore it, weaving my way through the crowd until I spill out on the other side of the cookout.

I don't have a headache. There's nothing wrong with me at all—except for my flushed skin and tightened belly. My

5

pounding heart, racing faster than it should for another man.

My bike leans against a battered brick wall, and I snatch up the handlebars with sweaty palms. I wobble as I swing a leg over—damn it, I only had two sips of beer—then I'm pushing off, pedaling hard as I join the road and build up speed. The wind whips at my cheeks, raking cool fingers through my hair, and it's a relief to push my legs until they burn. To do something with this nervous energy boiling under my skin.

It was nothing.

I'm making a fuss. But it was nothing.

That's easier to believe as I crest the last hill before home—my wonky second floor townhouse apartment on the edges of the town square. Back here, in the familiar streets and far from the manic energy of the lakeside, I can see this for what it was.

An overreaction.

So I felt a fleeting attraction to another man. So I panicked and scrambled out of there like a crazy person. So what? It doesn't mean anything, and god knows I would never act on a silly little crush. It's still Ezra I'm missing as I pull my bike to a stop, breathing hard as I shoulder the frame and carry it up the stone steps. It's *Ezra* I wish I'd invited back with me, to soothe my fake headache and spoon me on the couch.

It's Ezra I want. My boyfriend.

This is ridiculous. I can't freak out like this again.

Tomorrow I'll call Ezra. Make it up to him for running out like this—maybe do something fun and silly, like turn up at his place in nothing but a coat.

Next time there's a Mountain Rescue cookout, I'll keep my cool.

And I'll stay far, far away from Caleb Olsen.

# 2

# Ezra

*resent day*

P My fingertips turn white as I hang from the rock, teeth gritted in concentration. Far below, the crowd murmur as they watch, too afraid to shout out in case they put me off. Now and then, though, a gasp floats up to me when I execute a tricky move.

They're right to gasp. If they knew the real risks here, they'd *scream.*

I'm climbing without a rope.

This is reckless. So dangerous that my gut curdles with every gust of wind, every whispering breeze which threatens to tear me off the cliff face and fling me down to the jagged rocks below. But I'm up here now, committed to this climb, and second thoughts won't do shit for me eighty feet in the air. I'll have plenty of time to kick myself once I'm back on solid ground, and footage of this climb is winging its way around the internet.

They'll call me a hero and a madman by turns. I might even

7

get sponsorship offers.

None of that matters. My mom will fucking hate this.

Another woman crosses my mind, and I can't help myself. I wonder what Bianca will make of this climb—whether she'll be impressed, or horrified, or both.

Whether she'll feel anything at all.

Knowing Bianca, she'll have blocked any mention of me online. My ex-girlfriend is practical down to her steel core—as evidenced by the way she broke up with me one month ago. She'd already packed her things, written out a fucking speech with little note cards to make sure she hit every point she wanted.

How she loved me.

How grateful she was for our time together.

How she wished this could be different.

Fuck, I hated that speech.

A groan tears between my gritted teeth as I lunge upward, pushing off a tiny bump in the rock face for leverage. I can already feel my foot slipping when my fingers meet their next hold, clamping down and molding to its shape. I hang for a moment, my breath heaving in and out of me, and too late it occurs to me that if I fall, my best friend will be the one these spectators call.

Caleb is back at the Mountain Rescue office right now, waiting for the phone to ring with tales of trapped hikers and fallen logs in the road. The last thing he'll be ready for is news of *me*, splattered over the mountainside.

God, I'm an idiot. I scowl up at my route, pretending I don't notice the way my muscles are seizing, getting pumped from the effort of the climb. It's a simple enough route, at least—I'm not completely suicidal—but I should never have attempted it without a rope. Not at this time of year, when storms blow through the mountain ranges without warning and the rock is so cold, it freezes my fingers. It's *wet,* too, this high up, exposed to the elements, and I should have predicted that too.

So many things I should have done.

I push the thoughts of Bianca away again, a sour taste in my mouth.

There's a bailing point. A ledge jutting out ten feet up, two thirds up the cliff face. It slopes away, back into the mountain, and though it's still a risky climb, it's far better than this vertical route. Shrubs cling to the ledge, and though I don't trust them enough to use as a handhold, it's a good sign that they're there. Hopefully the ledge levels out, and I can make my way back to town with my pride dented but my body intact.

"Go on, Ezra!" Someone yells from below. Clearly, they didn't get the memo about letting me concentrate. The other spectators hush them, but that yell got me moving. I lunge forward again, bellowing between my teeth, and my heart nearly stops as the chunk of rock comes away in my hand.

"Heads!" I shout, even as I scramble to find another hold, my hand slipping desperately over the sheer rock face. I find a crack, jamming my fingers in the gap, and I'm so shocked by how close I came to death, I barely register the hot pain spreading over my knuckles.

When I catch my breath again, finally pulling my fingers free to reach for another hold, they come out red and ragged. I finish the climb with my throat clogged, my heart pumping so hard I can practically feel my chest moving. The crowd below groans in disappointment as I bail onto the sloping ledge, calling the route early, but fuck 'em. They're not the ones risking their lives.

My legs wobble all the way up the slope to the mountain path, and I tap every tree I walk past, like I'm counting my blessings or something. Counting handholds, maybe. Counting pieces of proof I'm still alive.

*Never again.* I promise myself as I wander down the rocky mountain path back toward town, even as a tiny voice whispers in the back of my head that I lived, didn't I? And if I hadn't bailed two-thirds of the way up, if I hadn't failed at this too, I'd be making headlines right now. Brands would be calling me by sundown, peppering me with offers. There would be interview requests. Trip invitations.

And Bianca might see.

Ah, goddamn it.

"You're an imbecile," I mutter to myself as my feet drum over the broken stone. My climbing shoes are thin soled, barely any protection, but I'm used to it. They're my second skin. Even when I step in a frozen puddle, lumps of ice floating on the surface, and soak through to my toes.

Yup. Sounds about right.

The wind moans through the trees, raising goosebumps where the sweat cools on the back of my neck, and I pick up the pace as I glance around. Storms come in fast out here, snap tantrums filled with ice and gale force winds, and I've had enough near-death experiences for one day. As the wind moans louder, trees cracking as they sway beside the path, I pick up to a jog. Little stones skitter away from my shoes, and my knuckles sting as I ball my hands into fists.

Enough feeling sorry for myself. Enough dramatics on the cliff face.

There's a storm coming.

Time to warn Mountain Rescue.

* * *

The town is empty as I jog through the streets. This time of year, the tourists have emptied out in search of warmer places, and the locals know better than to head out when a storm's brewing. Overhead, hands reach through open windows to close and bar wooden shutters, and across the street, the local butcher is closing up his shop early.

No point staying open on a day like this. Not when black clouds are gathering overhead, swirling over the rooftops, full-bellied with ice and rain. The temperature's dropping by the minute, my feet well and truly frozen now in my climbing shoes. I can barely feel them thumping against the sidewalk as I run, my toes like stones.

"Better head inside!" the butcher Jorge calls, pulling his rattling metal shutter down over his shop front. I raise a hand, too puffed after running down the mountain to call back, and wheel around the corner.

The Mountain Rescue headquarters stands across the square, the window glowing gold.

Home, sweet home.

The scratched front door swings open under my palm, a wall of heat swamping my cheeks. Caleb's a big man, but he's a sucker for warmth. Left to his own devices, he'd turn the office into a sauna.

"You there?" My voice bounces down the corridor. The bald carpet is scratchy underfoot—hell, if the cliff face had this much friction, I'd have swarmed up the route with no problem. On either side, cork noticeboards are plastered with fliers and community notices, and a weak bulb flickers overhead. "Caleb?"

11

I push the door to the reception area open and pause.

Caleb strides up and down the short length of the room, stymied at one end by the desk and at the other by a squashy brown sofa. He clips out instructions, one hand clutching a phone to his ear while he checks another in his palm. He glances over when I enter, dipping his chin in greeting, and I nod back as I shuffle fully into the room.

In here, with the light and the warmth and Caleb's low, rumbling voice, it hits me: I'm a mess. Soaked through and blue from the cold, dressed only in a long sleeved shirt and sweatpants. My knuckles look worse in the light, crusted with blood, the skin rucked up horribly.

I see the exact moment Caleb notices my hand. His brown eyes narrow, then drop to my climbing shoes, before climbing back to my own sheepish expression.

He rolls his eyes. Waves one phone at the first aid kit below the desk, then keeps pacing.

Alright, then.

*This* is where I should have come when I woke up missing Bianca so much, it was like a hole in my chest. Not to risk my life on a pointless climb. Here, to Caleb's quiet warmth and no-nonsense attitude.

My partner finishes up one call, tossing the phone onto his desk before he lifts the other to his ear. He picks up the thread of that conversation without pausing, though he strides over to the first aid kit where I've rested it on the desktop. He bats my hands away, his big paws so much larger than mine, and rummages for supplies.

"A crack?" he murmurs out of the corner of his mouth, a voice still buzzing through the handset against his ear. I nod. Caleb sighs, and tosses a roll of bandages onto the desk.

We fall into an easy routine as soon as he hangs up his call. Caleb plucks up my hand, turning it over and inspecting the damage in the light. His mouth twists, his tawny beard shifting, and I stare pointedly at the collar of his plaid shirt so I don't have to see his disappointed expression.

"You ran here, too."

"Yeah." I hiss as he cleans the wound and dabs antiseptic on my knuckles, the sting radiating up my arm. "Wanted to warn you there's a storm coming."

Caleb's eyes flick to the window over my shoulder. I turn too, grimacing at the heavy dark clouds and gusting winds. A newspaper flies past the window, pages flapping wildly and splotched with rain.

"There's a storm? No shit."

"Yeah, yeah, alright."

I can see why the folks who get banged up on the mountain always want Caleb taking care of them. He's precise in his movement, confident but gentle, and already my racing pulse is settling.

"Climbing in a storm." Caleb clicks his tongue. "That's risky, Ezra."

I wince. He doesn't know the half of it.

"I forgot to check the report."

Caleb grunts. He's right—that dumbass excuse doesn't even warrant a response. Not when I'm part of Mountain Rescue. I may not be full time anymore, not since my climbing took off, but I do enough shifts that I should know better.

"I was distracted," I offer. It's true, too. Since Bianca walked out last month, my thoughts have been snarled up in an impossible tangle. Days pass in a blur. I lose my keys every chance I get. I'm lucky if I don't forget my own name these days.

Caleb's eyes soften at the corners. He's still peering at my knuckles, wrapping them with a soft, white bandage, but something's changed. The subtle edge of reproach is gone.

"She'll figure it out," he says at last. And that's *not* what I need. False hope. Platitudes.

"Or she won't."

Caleb pauses, then nods. "Or she won't."

We stand there for a moment longer. Caleb's done wrapping my knuckles, but he still tilts my hand in the light, frowning at the pale lines of old scars on my skin.

My throat is dry when I tug my hand free. "Thanks, man."

Caleb's already turned, striding back to the desk. "No problem."

I should go home. For once, I'm not on shift tonight, since Caleb is paired with Beau Walker. I can hear Beau's voice rumbling through the wall—rough around the edges, like the older man barely talks except when he's here. They've got this covered.

But my clothes are still damp, my limbs chilled beneath the fabric, and the last fucking thing I want is to run through that icy wind back to my cold, empty apartment.

"Hey, Caleb." I stare out of the window. The light's fading. "Have I always been this tragic?"

A snort. Pages flipping. "Probably."

I grin as I flop into a chintzy armchair, stretching my legs out in front of a spluttering space heater.

I may be tragic.

But at least I'm gonna be warm.

# 3

# Bianca

Holy shit, it's cold.
And windy.
And *wet.*
Can't a girl catch a damn break?

Coming up onto the mountain in February was a last resort. A desperate measure, when catching glimpses of Ezra and—and *him*—around town every day got to be too much. Every time I saw one of them, it was like a kick to the stomach. I was left gasping for breath; completely winded.

And when they both inevitably turned away from me, their expressions shuttered...

God, it hurt. Even though I deserve all that and worse.

This is the downside of living in a small town. It's not the summer tourists, nor the lack of take-out options. It's *this*: being completely unable to escape my ex boyfriend and his best friend. I can't even complain about it to anyone, because I'm the one who left Ezra.

Never mind that it was the worst day of my life.

So while I never thought a few weeks up on the peaks

would be *relaxing*, I figured, hey—at least I'd get some privacy. Somewhere to lick my wounds away from their cool gaze. Somewhere to be sad without reproach. And I got my wish in the form of my coworker Stacey's old cabin.

Draped in cobwebs and falling into disrepair, the cabin is exactly as gross as she warned me.

"No one's been up there for three seasons," she'd said, twirling the key around her knuckle. "Are you sure?"

"Stacey. You angel. I'm sure."

I'd snatched that rusted key like it was the secret to eternal life. And when I hiked for hours, thighs burning, to reach this tumbledown wreck…

Well, she warned me. And I am determined to make this work. I dropped my backpack in the doorway and didn't even rest my aching feet before scrounging up a broom and chasing out the biggest spiders. Next went the dried leaf litter, blown through a gaping hole in one wall. I swept all that crap out, then set my shoulder against a heavy wooden bookcase and shoved until it covered the hole.

Great builder, I am not. But at least now the wind doesn't blow *directly* into my face where I'm huddled on the dusty bed, swaddled in every blanket I could find.

"This is perfect." My teeth chatter as I mutter to myself—clearly a sign that I'm going mad. "The perfect place to nurse a broken heart."

There *is* a romantic sort of poetry to the cabin. Though it's fallen into disrepair, it has the skeleton of a gorgeous old building. All the furniture is solid and well made—maybe even hand carved by one of Stacey's relations—and the fire crackling merrily in the log burner washes everything with a soft glow. The bookcase is laden with old classics and cowboy books, and

I even found a stack of faded comics under the wooden table.

It has potential. It's *pre*-cozy.

That's what I'm telling myself, anyway.

A sudden gust of wind slams against the side of the cabin, rattling a row of mugs on their shelf and sending sawdust showering down from the ceiling. I watch, open mouthed, as the heavy bookcase rocks on its base, pushed solely by the wind, several paperbacks dropping onto the floorboards.

"Oh my god."

I lunge to my feet, blankets still clutched around my shoulders like a cape. The wind howls louder, louder than the wolves I pretended I didn't hear last night, and the bookcase rocks so far, I think for *sure* it's going to fall. Books drop onto the floorboards in a steady, thumping drip, and finally my brain comes back online and urges my feet to move.

My blankets slip off my shoulders, pooling forgotten on the faded rug as I grit my teeth and drag the heavy wooden table jerking over the floorboards. It's heavy, dragging on my arm sockets, and when I finally wedge it up against the bookcase, my cheeks are warm and I'm sweating under my goosebumps.

The wind howls.

The bookcase rocks.

The table stands steady.

"Good." I pat the gnarled wooden surface, polished by dozens of hands over the years. "That works. Thank you."

My blankets crackle with fragments of dried leaves as I scoop them up. I shake them out, nose wrinkled against the dust, then wrap them quickly around my shoulders again before flopping back onto the bed.

It's just some wind. A bit of bad weather.

Nothing to worry about.

17

\* \* \*

My mom taught me a trick when I was a little girl and our heat went out one winter. First, she bundled me up in blankets. Tucked a hot water bottle by my feet. I mean, she's not an idiot.

But then, she told me to close my eyes and think about the warmest place I could imagine. Back then, it was a tropical island, with coconut trees and white sands and a pirate ship bobbing in the distance. And Mom said to picture it all: the warmth of sunshine on my skin, the baking hot breeze, the sensation of being too hot in my clothes.

I opened my eyes, and I was *thirsty*. Got cold again after a while, but it was nice while it lasted.

Bundled up in my icy cabin, I figure I'll try anything to thaw out my frozen feet. They're chunky with three thick layers of socks, and I still can't feel my toes as I crawl inside my sleeping bag, piled high with blankets on the narrow bed.

I flop onto my back. Blink up at the ceiling, with narrow strips of evening sky visible through the holey roof.

"Alright. *Warm.* Warm thoughts, Bianca."

The tropical island isn't gonna cut it.

Casting my mind back over the last few years, the hottest day I can remember was a day spent climbing with Ezra. It was high summer, unusually hot for Lonely Mountain, and we were exposed to the sun in a valley. Ezra was stripped to the waist—he likes to climb shirtless, the show-off—and his muscled chest and toned arms were seriously distracting. He kept catching me staring, and he was so thrilled every time, laughing and prodding my ribs.

He was just as bad, though. Especially when I drew my long brown hair up into a ponytail. His gaze snagged on the curve of my neck; on the hollow of my collarbone. And when he took me to the rock face, dusting our hands with chalk and showing me how to tie onto the rope, he kept finding excuses to touch me.

He stood behind me, linking our fingers together before showing me different holds on the rock.

He checked the buckles of my harness. Stole a quick inhale of my neck.

That was an early date. So early, we were still shy around each other. Unsure but so excited.

I screw my eyes shut harder, tears spilling into my hair.

Yeah. That valley with Ezra. That's the warmest memory I have.

The cliff sides funneled the sunshine down to us, catching us in a heat sink. And it got so hot, we both burned, and I *never* burn. Every breath was warm and dry as it passed through my throat, and my top stuck to my skin by the time we were done climbing. Ezra shot up that wall like a mountain goat, while I puffed and struggled my way to the first ledge.

I shift in my sleeping bag, the bed creaking under my weight. Maybe it's in my head, or maybe it's the blankets, but I feel a little better. Part thawed, even as my chest aches. When I wriggle my toes, I think maybe I can feel the thick wool of my socks.

Clearing my throat, I try to hold onto that memory again. The laughter; the shy glances. The shiver of insects in the long grass. But, inevitably, my brain tracks away from Ezra to another man. This is a well-worn pathway in my head, worn smooth like a riverbed after I've followed it so many times.

I'm weak. But it's impossible to picture warmth without thinking about Caleb Olsen.

Maybe it's the copper strands in his hair, or his gentle chuckle. Maybe it's those soft flannel shirts he always wears—so criminally cozy that all I want to do is bury my nose in the center of his chest and inhale. It would be different than Ezra's chest. Caleb is bulky where Ezra is wiry; padded where Ezra is rock hard.

I huff loudly, burying deeper into my sleeping bag.

Even here, I can't escape them.

But… as my hands roam idly under the covers, brushing over my stomach, something else heats my blood. I came up here to forget them, yes, but this is an emergency, right? Survival of the thirstiest. And my body responds to this far more than my little mind games, heat crackling through my frozen limbs. My cheeks burn where they meet the icy air above the lip of my sleeping bag, and I bite my lip as I let my hands wander.

Lower… lower…

My fingertips dip inside my leggings.

There's no excuse for this. For the thoughts that have haunted my waking hours since I first met Caleb at the cookout. My only saving grace is that Ezra is always there too in my daydreams, when I let my mind truly go free. Touching me. Kissing *him*. And then Caleb's big hands span my waist and *squeeze.*

I whimper.

Thank god there's no one here to see this. The locals in town know me as a practical young woman. Endlessly pragmatic; never showing undue emotion. I rule the lakeside summer camp with the strictness of a school matron.

Now I'm dipping my fingers between my legs, tears streaming into my hair as I think about the two men I can't have.

*Crash.*

The sound of shattering glass jolts me upright, my legs

20

trapped in my narrow sleeping bag. My pile of blankets slides sideways onto the floor, and I stare across the cabin, my heart slamming in my chest.

Broken glass litters the floorboards, glinting in the glow cast by the log burner.

And punched through the shattered window, a tree branch stretches towards me across the room.

I blink. Wait with held breath for the cabin to collapse with me in it. Count backwards from one hundred, mind racing. What is there to do? I can't fix the window—not right now.

I flop back onto the bed with a groan. Shivering again.

This goddamn wind.

# 4

# Caleb

There are three phones in the Mountain Rescue HQ, and none of them have fallen quiet for more than a minute this shift. It's a nightmare—a classic Lonely Mountain storm, where the weather whips in with zero warning and leaves a trail of destruction behind it. You'd think we'd be used to it, living here. Hell—I grew up in this town before I moved away at sixteen. But somehow it's still a shock every time the mountain takes a hit at us, gathering storm clouds and striking at the trees with bolts of lightning.

This one's worse than usual, too.

Someone has truly pissed off the mountain.

I hang up on one call and immediately pick up another, watching Ezra out of the corner of my eye. He's slumped on the sofa by the window, his clothes drying out by the heater even as his skin stays way too pale. His eyes are closed, his head tipped back against the sofa, and exhaustion is clear in every line on his sculpted face.

Ezra. He shouldn't even be here right now—I'm on shift with Beau Walker, not him. But he ran here with busted knuckles to

22

warn me about the storm.

Ezra's loyal.

And I don't deserve it.

"You got a survival kit?" I talk to the lady on the phone, her voice high and strangled in my ear. She's scared, but she's fine. Her place is on the outskirts of town—it's the folks up on the mountain or by the river banks who need to worry. "A flashlight? Bottled water? Uh-huh."

She babbles in my ear, reeling off a list of her supplies, and I half listen. This lady, she calls us every time there's a single rain cloud. She's not practical at all, nothing like—

I shut that thought down, rubbing at my chest. Nope, not going there.

Even with them broken up, Bianca's still off limits.

The office door opens behind me, and I lower my voice, talking our caller down from her panic as Beau and a strange man come into the room. The stranger is battered, hobbling on crutches, with sickly old bruises and dried out cuts decorating his pale face. He looks young—mid twenties, maybe—and he keeps his head ducked, choosing his path carefully across the rug.

He's the ultimate contrast to Beau. Slender and clean shaven where Beau's big and bearded. Ghostly pale next to Beau's light brown skin.

"Sit there," Beau rumbles, pointing at the sofa next to Ezra's sleeping form. He nods at me, his steps heavy as he rounds the desk and peers at the map on the wall.

Beau's friend looks up as he lowers to the sofa, and I get a shock of recognition as I stare into his ice chip eyes.

It's the hiker. The guy we rescued a while back from the river bed.

23

Angelo, or something.

"Must be bring your friend to work day," I murmur to Beau once I've turned back to the desk. Beau grunts, lifting one shoulder.

"Not my friend."

"Then why…?"

Beau gusts out a sigh, the floorboards creaking as he steps closer to the map.

"He's staying in my cabin. Not safe in the storm."

"…Right." I peer back at the new guy with fresh curiosity. He holds my gaze, shameless, and when he cocks his head, I get the weirdest feeling. Like even though I'm bigger, I'm a mouse squaring off with a cobra.

A shiver runs down my spine.

The phone ringing on the desk jolts me back to earth, and I turn and get back to work. It's always a slog, coordinating the storm efforts. I'd rather be out there, hiking out to injured climbers and carrying out emergency repairs, not talking on the damn phone. There's nothing like the rush of being out there in person, feeling the icy rain slicking down your neck and hearing the thunder rumble overhead. Adrenaline coursing through your muscles, even as your breaths come calm.

But I'm in charge today, which means when our first call comes in, it's Beau who gets to plunge out into the storm. I juggle the calls and move pins across the map, our radios crackling with updates from the teams on the mountain.

"You'd make a great secretary."

Ezra's awake, then.

I snort. "You think?"

"Hell yeah. I can see it now." He shifts on the sofa, nudging the bruised guy perched next to him. "Cute tortoiseshell glasses.

Tight little pencil skirt. You see it?"

"I see it." Angelo speaks quietly, with a slight accent. Italian, maybe.

"Shut up." I grimace, the tips of my ears burning. Ezra's always doing this. Pushing me, taunting me. Stopping just this side of flirting.

He doesn't know what it does to me.

"You're the climber," the guy says suddenly. "I saw your video earlier."

Ezra clears his throat, and for the first time, looks kind of shifty. I turn back to the map, ears straining to listen.

"It was nothing."

"No, it was impressive. Climbing without a rope—"

"For fuck's sake." Ezra winces as I wheel around. There are very few things that piss me off in this world, but Ezra's goddamn stupid risk-taking is right up there. A tinny voice chatters away from the phone by my ear, but I'm not listening anymore.

Goddamn Ezra. "Are you serious right now?"

Angelo raises an eyebrow. "This would be a strange thing to lie about. Don't you think?"

"Fuck. *Fuck.*" I hold the phone up, then growl when I hear the line's dead. It rattles as I slam it back in the cradle. "Jesus Christ, Ezra. Are you trying to kill me?"

"Obviously not."

"Then why—"

He holds his palms up, warding me off, but irritation flashes in his green eyes. "It was dumb, okay? It won't happen again. So back off, man."

*Back off.*

I ought to drop kick this idiot up the mountain.

25

I open my mouth, ready to rip into him again, but something catches my eye through the window. The town square is dark, the thunderclouds blocking out so much daylight that it looks almost night time. Rain lashes past the glass, glinting silvery in the light from the office, and running across the square is a wide eyed, bedraggled woman.

She skids to a halt at our door, arms pinwheeling, and shoves it open with a bang. There's a thump in the corridor as she bounces off a wall, and then one soaked camp counselor stands in our office, chest heaving and pixie cut spiked up with rain.

"Stacey? What's wrong?"

Lonely Mountain only has a few towns, and this is the biggest. Everyone knows everyone around here.

Besides, Stacey works at the lakeside camp with Bianca. And anything to do with Bianca sticks way too easily in my brain.

"Sh—She…" Stacey doubles over, propping her hands on her knees as she catches her breath. Behind her, Angelo smirks from the sofa.

"Sit down," Ezra offers, leaping up, but Stacey shakes her head. And when she speaks again, she directs it at him, even though I'm the one in charge.

"It's Bianca." Ezra's face falls. He freezes, one arm still stretched towards the sofa. "She's in my family's cabin. Up on the mountain." Stacey turns to me finally, her eyes pleading. "It's a wreck. And it's so exposed. There's no phone, no generator, nothing. If the storm caught her off guard…"

"We'll take care of it," I rasp. My throat is suddenly so dry.

Bianca. Out there. Up on the mountain, exposed to *this*.

I have to find her.

\* \* \*

26

"I'm going." Ezra follows me to the lockers in the next room, yanking his own open and pulling out his spare boots and jacket. "You stay here and man the phones."

Yeah, that's not happening. This Angelo guy can play secretary for a while. Just until Beau gets back.

"You're not even on shift. And you've busted your hand."

Ezra scoffs, kicking his climbing shoes off and shoving his feet into his boots. The hard line of his jaw is stark, even in the gloomy locker room. The light bulb is weak overhead, and the room is draped in shadows and smells stale with the musk of old clothes.

"Ezra." He kneels, tying a boot with stiff, fumbling fingers. Pretending like he doesn't even hear me. "You can't come. You know you can't. You're not objective when it comes to Bianca."

He stills, mouth twisting. "And you are?"

My heart slams against my rib cage. I stare down at my best friend, kneeling on the dusty locker room floor and glaring up at me in challenge.

I thought I hid it well. Every time they kissed in front of me and I practically cracked open with yearning; each time she called my name and my heart skipped a beat. I buried all of it, every impulse to reach for her, to *claim* her—I shoved it down deep and tried to be a better man.

Someone who doesn't pine after his best friend's girl.

And clearly I did a shitty job, but Ezra's never done this. Never called me out before for my fucking blatant crush on his girlfriend.

My eyes must have followed her around every room, sheer longing painted on my face.

Did they both know? Did they laugh about it?

"I—I don't—"

27

There's no excuse. Nothing I can say in my defense.

"It's fine. Okay? It doesn't fucking matter, especially not anymore. But I'm going after her, and you of all people will not stop me."

His bitter tone is a punch to the gut.

"Ezra." He pushes to his feet and shrugs on his jacket, not looking me in the eye. Shame clogs my throat, but I force the words out, grabbing his sleeve as he shoves past. "*Ezra.* I'm not—I won't deny it. Okay? You're right. We both know you are. I tried to ignore it and I sure as hell hoped to hide it, but here we are. I've—I've fucked up. But Mountain Rescue is my *job*, and I'm good at it, and I care about her too, whether you like that fact or not."

His jaw works. I can almost hear his teeth grinding. So I go against my better judgment.

"We'll both go. Alright?"

Ezra huffs again, still not looking at me, but he nods once, sharp. I drop his sleeve.

"And I'm sorry," I croak as he pushes back through the office doorway. "About—about Bianca."

I don't know what I'm apologizing for, exactly. It's not like I ever said anything, and I'm sure as hell not the reason she left him last month. I'm not a total piece of shit—I'd never make a play for someone else's girl. I liked her, that's all, just like he did, and I respected their relationship. Never tried to interfere.

But I *am* sorry. And queasy with shame.

"I know," Ezra mutters as he strides out, the door falling shut behind him. I stand there for ten long seconds, my insides raw, breathing in the dust motes spinning through the air. He's my best friend. My partner. And though he doesn't seem to notice it, he's the *other* person who lives rent free in my brain.

Seeing Ezra glare at me like that, like he didn't even know me...

It's not a sight I ever want to see again. But I square my shoulders and follow after, bracing myself for more sharp words.

Bianca needs us. I'd weather a hell of a lot worse for her.

# 5

# Ezra

The truck lurches over a pothole, the wipers working frantically to clear the rain and sleet from the glass. I grip the handle above the passenger window, jaw clenched so hard my teeth ache as I stare out into the storm.

It's chaos. The worst we've seen in years.

And Bianca's out there somewhere. Hurt, maybe, or scared, or god knows what else.

"Can you go any faster?" I grit out, still not looking at Caleb. I can't see that hurt reproach, that guilty alarm in his eyes again. I should never have called him out for wanting her. Not when he never acted on it, and especially not when I lost all hold over her a month ago. It's not like I can blame him. She's fucking magic.

I'm still not sorry.

"It's the tires." His voice is so low, it's almost lost beneath the crackling thunder and the rain pounding on the truck roof. Caleb wrenches the gear stick, a muscle ticking in his temple as he scowls up the mountain pass. "The road's turned to shit."

Another shape looms out of the darkness: Beau's truck,

coming back from his rescue. An elderly woman hunkers in the passenger seat beside the huge man, swaddled in a tartan blanket, and I don't know what she's more scared of: the storm or her driver. She darts him wide-eyed glances, lingering on his thick, dark beard, one gnarled hand clutching the truck door like she might commando roll out at any moment.

Their truck lumbers past, rocking on the uneven path, and Beau nods at us from behind his fogged windshield.

"Come on," I mutter under my breath. Bianca's *out there.*

"Not helpful."

"I know. Just... come *on.*"

A wrinkled map is spread over the dash, with Stacey's family cabin marked with a rushed X. I stare at that pencil mark like I might teleport us there by sheer force of will, until my eyes go fuzzy and a headache throbs at the base of my skull. And we rock and lurch up the flooded mountain path, the water rushing past the tires getting deeper until floating logs and debris slam into the doors.

"The river must've burst." Caleb wipes his forehead on his sleeve, still scowling forward. "I can get us a tiny bit closer, then we'll have to go on foot. The flood should get better as we climb."

As soon as the words leave his mouth, lightning spears through the darkness, lighting up the sky a brilliant white. Thunder rolls through straight after, so loud my ears pop.

"Yeah, okay." I shift in my recently dried clothes. "Whatever it takes."

What it *takes* is another ten minutes of the truck tires churning, the engine screaming for relief, until Caleb pulls over. If I needed any sign that he cared about her too, this is it: Caleb loves that truck. But he ditches it at the side of the road without a backward glance, shouldering his backpack with the rescue kit and snatching the map off the dash.

"Stay close," he grunts. "Don't wanna rescue you both."

I wind the truck window down and slide out into the flood. Icy water fills my boots and soaks my pants to my thighs. "Aw, Caleb. That's so sweet."

His words might have rankled, but honestly, it's a relief to wade in his slipstream. Caleb's *big,* a hulking mass of a man, and even though I like to pretend I've never noticed, his body is useful now. I follow close behind him, mirroring his movements to lessen the chance of stepping into a pothole. Caleb surges forward, an unstoppable force moving through the storm, and after a brief pause, I grab a fistful of the back of his shirt.

He grunts—whether in approval or irritation, I don't know. I hold on tighter.

And duck my head against the storm.

The thing is: I'm a climber. I'm no stranger to hiking up mountains—the best rock faces are up there, tucked away out of reach. I wander up Lonely Mountain more days than not, and I do it with a heavy kit bag slung over my shoulders, packed full of climbing ropes and clunky metal gear.

There's nothing on my back now, but my thighs still scream at the effort of wading against the current. I already put my body through hell once today, and now I'm paying the price. My busted hand throbs where it's clutched to my chest—another reminder of my dumb decisions—and I can't feel my feet in the icy water.

"Bank up ahead!" Caleb yells, his voice snatched away but the wind, but I follow his outstretched arm.

A bank. Steep sided, with tree roots jutting out of the soil.

And above them: sweet, sweet dry land.

Caleb pushes me up first, then hands the backpack up after. I wait as he climbs up, kind of ungainly in his size, but he's not breathing half as hard as I am when he stands next to me, dripping onto the dirt.

He's made for this.

Shit, I'm glad he's here.

Caleb takes the backpack without another word, shoulders it, then sets off through the trees.

* * *

We find her as night falls. It's already so dark from the storm, you might not see the difference, except for the waxy moon peeking through the gaps in the clouds. Stacey's cabin is worse than I pictured: a ruined shack of a building with holes in the roof and a corrugated metal outhouse. The moonlight casts a silvery glow over the wooden boards, and I'm relieved to see a faint line of light under the door as we hike closer.

"Maybe I should go first."

I whip around to face Caleb. *What the hell?*

He shrugs, mouth pressed in a firm line. "She might not want to see you, man."

I start to curse him out, call him the worst names I can think of, but the truth of his words holds me back. It's true. Bianca might not want to see me—even in a life-threatening storm.

She left me, after all.

"What am I supposed to do? Wait in the rain like a dog?"

Caleb winces. "Just let me knock. I'll warn her first, okay?"

I swipe at a tree trunk with my bad hand, hissing at it makes contact. *Fuck.* He's right.

"Okay. Yeah, fine."

Should I not have come? Maybe we're not together anymore, but I'm still allowed to care about her, right? For a horrible, sinking moment I picture a cool expression when she opens the door. Empty dismissal in her expressive eyes.

But then lightning flashes again, cracking against a tree nearby and sending a shower of red sparks to the ground.

Screw it. Bianca can hate me if she wants. But I'm making sure she's *safe.*

My back flattens against the side of the cabin as Caleb thumps on the door, rapping hard to be heard above the wind and thunder. All around, trees are bowed against the force of the gale, the storm's destruction already littering the mountainside with branches and bits of debris.

We wait. My heart squeezes in my chest.

Caleb curses and knocks again, louder.

Light bursts through the doorway as it wrenches open, a rectangle of firelight bathing Caleb in its glow. Sheer relief coasts over his features as he takes her in, eyes hungry, and suddenly I can't wait out of sight anymore.

"Caleb," I hear Bianca say, and fuck, she sounds so thrilled to see him. "How did you—"

I move into sight. The words freeze in her mouth.

She's disheveled. Bundled up with blankets; soaked through and wide-eyed with fear.

But as my ex-girlfriend takes me in, gaze darting to the man at my side and back, my heart sinks. She's tensing up. All that relief I just heard is gone.

"Oh." Bianca coughs, holding the corner of a blanket over her mouth. Then she forces a smile. "Ezra. Hi."

34

# 6

# Bianca

Either this is a bad dream, or the two men I'm trying to get away from... are here.

Standing outside Stacey's family cabin. Soaked through with their eyebrows raised, waiting for me to invite them inside.

*Crap.*

I yank the door open wider, waving my ex boyfriend and the reason I left him over the threshold. A small, petty part of me wants to slam the door in their faces. Opt out of this whole freaking encounter. But there's a storm raging, and I've never been the rude type.

"Do you guys, uh.... want coffee? I could boil water."

As soon as the words out, I wish I could stuff them back in my mouth. This isn't a *social call.* And I'm not playing host—not in a ruined cabin with a hole in the wall and a tree branch punched through one window. Ezra rounds the pool of broken glass, glittering in the firelight, and prods a shard with the toe of his boot.

"Love what you've done with the place, Bee."

Right.

"Why are you here?" I gather the blankets tighter around my shoulders, my clothes wet and clammy where they cling to my skin.

"For that coffee," Ezra deadpans, voice flat. Caleb shoots him a look, then talks over him.

"Mountain Rescue. Because of the storm."

I cast a doubtful look over the pair of them. Sure, they're both strong, imposing guys. Even Ezra, who's a few inches shorter and narrower than Caleb, is well muscled and broad shouldered from all the climbing. But they're drenched, faces pale from the cold, and a blood soaked bandage is wrapped around Ezra's hand. Their clothes are torn and they're both breathing hard.

Honestly, they look less like rescuers and more like refugees.

"The road flooded. We came on foot."

"Okay..." I shake my head, trying to make sense of this. "That doesn't explain why *you're* here."

Ezra scoffs, striding closer, and I wince at his mocking gaze. He's handsome and charismatic, a true showman when he needs to be, but he can be viciously sharp too when he feels like it.

"Don't flatter yourself. We were on shift, that's all."

Caleb's mouth twists, but he says nothing. And the man I loved—the man I *still* love—pushes on. He's gaining speed, each word hurled at me like a missile.

"You think we dropped everything and came chasing up the mountain because it's you? Wishful thinking, princess. We came because it's our job. Not because we give a shit."

"Ezra—" Caleb mutters.

I shake my head. Let him get this out.

"The truth is, there are a hundred fucking places I'd rather be

36

than here. A hundred people I'd rather come for. But you had to take risks, didn't you? What—were you missing the attention?"

I tip my chin mutely, waiting for him to finish. And finally, finally, Ezra runs out of steam. He trails off, watching me with hard eyes, before his shoulders slump.

Silence rings through the cabin, broken only by the wind moaning outside. I clear my throat.

"The storm wasn't on the forecast. I apologize for the inconvenience."

Caleb steps forward. "You're soaked. You went outside?"

"Yes. I tried to make my way down not long ago."

"Too rough out there?"

I nod, annoyed. If I'd known *they'd* be coming, I would have tried harder to fight my way down. Anything to avoid this disaster of a conversation. "I slipped in all the mud. Went over a short drop."

Ezra makes a small noise, but Caleb doesn't even look at him. I don't think I've ever seen him dismiss his friend like that. "You need first aid?"

I consider the shallow cuts and grazes along my side. No point being a martyr.

"Please."

It's a relief to let Caleb usher me across the room. He herds me to the bed—there's no sofa—and slings a backpack onto the mattress.

Ezra watches as his partner pulls out a first aid kit. Unwraps my blankets and lifts the hem of my shirt with gentle hands. And his scoff echoes around the cabin before he storms out, slamming the door shut behind him.

I curl in on myself, my heart aching and raw, and kind, brown eyes flick to mine.

"Let him cool down," Caleb murmurs. His fingertips probe along my rib cage, searching for fractures and blazing a burning trail along my skin. Even kneeling on the floorboards, he looms over me, blocking out the firelight.

"He hates me." My voice is so pathetically small. "All that time together…"

"He doesn't hate you."

I bark a laugh, but there's no humor in it. "Were we just in the same room?"

Caleb tilts his head, considering, as his fingers sweep higher. Higher.

Then, decision made, he leans closer. My breath stills.

"Bianca? Ezra wasn't on shift. He wanted to come."

\* \* \*

Caleb Olsen has a golden touch. I can't pin down why—the palms of his hands are rough and callused; his fingers are meaty; he's more strength than grace. But as he works his way along the cuts and grazes down my side, it's almost as relaxing as a massage.

Except when he applies the antiseptic. That stings like hell.

"You have to give him time."

Oh, and he won't stop talking about Ezra. That kind of stings, too. But it's familiar—every single time we've been alone since meeting a year and a half ago, Caleb has turned the conversation to his best friend.

It's like an evasive maneuver. Like if he doesn't bring Ezra up, I might talk about the elephant in the room: the tension crackling between us.

It's always been like this. Darting glances; held breaths. And

I felt so freaking *guilty*. So I walked away.

As if I'm going to drag that all up now. Caleb can relax—he's safe from me.

"Sure. Well, that's easier to do when he doesn't track me up a mountain."

"He was worried about you."

"I'm fine."

"And we're both glad about that."

I steal a glance at the man kneeling over me. Caleb *never* talks about himself. Only Ezra.

"Were *you* on shift?" I hate myself for asking, but I can't help it. I need to know.

The fire pops in the log burner. "Yes."

"Oh."

His mouth twists. And the words sounds dragged out of him when he admits: "But I'd have come either way, too."

My heart splutters back to life. If things were simpler, this would be everything I wanted—everything I left Ezra for.

But there's still something missing.

Still *someone* missing.

I never stopped wanting Ezra. I want them *both*.

"Why did you leave him?" Caleb frowns at his hands, dabbing antiseptic over a graze on my hip. There's an unspoken question there, hanging in the air between us. Something guilty, but tinged with hope.

He's a coward. So am I.

"You know why." He does. It's part of the problem—we've always understood each other perfectly. Never had to say the words. The wind gusts against the side of the cabin, rattling the wooden boards and making me jump. "I tried to ignore it; tried waiting for it to fade. But it wasn't going anywhere, Caleb.

Not for me. And it wasn't fair on Ezra. He's a good guy. He deserves someone's undivided attention."

Caleb nods, mouth pinched, and goes back to his work. And I stare at the wall, throat working.

Caleb deserves that too. And I can't offer it to either of them.

It's a relief when Ezra comes back, practically kicking the door open. Snowflakes billow inside with him—the temperature must be dropping, freezing the rain in the clouds. He gives us a sour look, then goes to coax the flames in the log burner higher. His shoulders are rigid with tension, his back turned to us, but even his anger is better than his absence.

God, I've missed him so much.

But I couldn't tell him before. Couldn't face how I felt. Couldn't stand the guilt, the constant risk of hurting him.

So I did the right thing.

I *did.*

# 7

# Caleb

I haven't been alone with Bianca since New Year's Eve. And I should *not* know that, should not keep track of my best friend's girlfriend, practically crossing the days without seeing her off a calendar.

Well... his *ex*-girlfriend.

It doesn't matter. She's still off limits.

She looked amazing that night. She always does, whether she's trussed up in her summer camp manager uniform or relaxed in denim shorts and a baggy t-shirt. At New Year's, Bianca wore a rare dress—a simple purple tunic with thick leggings underneath, and her dark hair braided over one shoulder. When we somehow found ourselves alone together for half an hour, huddling outside a friend's front porch to get away from the crowd for a while, I couldn't take my eyes off her.

So Ezra's right to shoot me a poisonous glare as he comes back inside.

He sees it all. He always has.

It never used to bother him—not outwardly, anyway—but

I guess all that changed when Bianca walked away. Now his green eyes are narrowed with distrust when they fall on me. He's wondering if I did something. Said something. Made this happen.

"Road's fucked," Ezra says, tone short. "The mud's freezing. Rain's turned to snow." He scowls at the pair of us, sitting too close together, then crosses to tend the log burner. "With the light gone, it's too risky. We're in for the night."

"Great," Bianca mutters, so quiet only I can hear. "The perfect sleepover."

No kidding. Bet she's thrilled we came after her.

I'm not sorry. Maybe she didn't need us, but we couldn't be sure until we came. And neither of us were willing to take any chances.

I push to my feet, pulling out my phone to try and get through to Beau. I've ditched my post, but whatever happens, he'll be able to handle it. The man's cut from these mountains. He's a force of nature. So I'm not worried as we talk, the sounds of the office faint through the handset.

Across the cabin, Bianca and Ezra watch each other warily.

*Do it*, I will them privately. *Talk it out. Make this work.*

They were so freaking happy. I can't be the person who ruined that. Especially not by mistake, without even knowing I was in the way. Bitterness churns in my stomach—bitterness that Bianca couldn't let it go. Couldn't let them be happy.

"Thanks, Beau. Call me with an update."

Without his voice in my ear, I've got nothing between me and the thick tension in the room. Bianca and Ezra are both silent, scowling at opposite walls, and the hiss and spit of the log burner is the only other sound.

"So." I sound off, even to myself. Fake and awkward. "How

shall we do this? Sleep in shifts? Keep an eye on the storm?"

It's barely dinnertime, but I'd do anything to escape this tension. And the others must feel the same way, because they nod quickly too.

"Yep."

"Sounds good."

"I'll take first shift."

"I'll sleep on the rug."

Dismayed, Bianca watches Ezra tug a single thin blanket off the bed and drop onto the floor, rolling over with his back to her. Squaring her shoulders, she turns to me. Raises her chin.

"What about you, Caleb?"

*The bed. Please, the bed.*

"I'm good here."

She nods once, sharp. Then draws her knees up, rests her chin on her legs, and stares out the broken window.

Message received. There was an offer, and I blew it.

I sit down heavily, lean my back against the wall, and let my eyes drift closed.

\* \* \*

I've shot to my feet, breathing hard and eyes wide, before my brain registers what's going on. The crash was so loud, the echoes still hanging in the air, and the glow of the firelight is gone. The cabin is filled with velvet darkness, and two sets of quick breaths cut through the quiet alongside mine.

"Ezra?" Bianca's voice shakes. She sounds so tiny, in the darkness by the wall.

"I'm here. I'm okay."

What the hell happened? I dig the heel of my palm into one

43

eye, shuffling carefully across the floorboards. Shards of glass crackle under my boots, the boards creaking with my weight, and one hand stretches in front of my face, feeling for obstacles.

"The fire…"

Ezra grunts. "Something came through the roof. Took the log burner out."

He was close to the burner. Curled on his side on the rug. Panic gnaws at my gut—sickly fear that he's hurt—but no. He's talking to us. Shifting slowly over the floor, patting his way toward the bed.

"You hurt?"

My voice is brusque. Like I'm offering him a beer. Like I don't *care.*

"No. I'm good. Just some embers landed on my arm."

Shit. "You need first aid?"

He snorts, and then I know he's fine. "No, Mom."

"Ass."

He laughs again, bright and loud. And even though this situation is anything but funny, a grin stretches my cheeks as I shuffle toward the sound of their voices.

"Bianca?"

"Yeah?"

"There's a flashlight in my backpack."

"Oh. Right." She scrabbles in the darkness, tugging my heavy backpack across the mattress. There's the tug of a zipper, soft curses under her breath, and then the light flicks on, shining bright in my eyes. "Sorry! Sorry." The beam lowers to the ground. All three of us blink in the sudden glare.

"No problem."

White spots float in my vision, but I can still make out Bianca huddled in her sleeping bag on the bed, her dark waves tangled around her shoulders, and Ezra crouched close to her side. His hand stretches over the mattress, reaching for her, and when he sees me staring, he snatches it back. Settles on his heels, the humor draining from his face.

"Guess we're in for a cold night."

Understatement of the century. Without the heat from the log burner, the temperature's dropping fast in the cabin. Snowflakes swirl in through the hole in the roof, ghostly in the patchy moonlight, and our breaths crystallize in frosty clouds in front of our chins.

"Shit."

"Yeah."

Bianca leans forward, propping the flashlight up in the folds of her blankets so that it points steadily at the opposite wall. The beam casts stark shadows over Ezra's face, hollowing his cheekbones and darkening his eyes, and I halt when I realize he's shaking. Already shuddering from the cold.

Of course he is. His clothes were soaked, and he only had that one threadbare blanket. Me, I've got padding, a burly furnace of a body, but Ezra is all hard muscles and lean limbs. No body fat on him.

"Get in the bed." My tone brooks no argument. "Bianca, shuffle up for him. He's freezing."

She looks at him, alarmed, moving over so fast she nearly kicks the flashlight off the bed. It bobs, the beam dipping up and down the wall.

"I'm fine."

"Bullshit." I stride over, the broken glass forgotten. "Don't be an ass. Get in the damn bed."

Bianca's sleeping bag comes undone with a swift tug on the zipper. She realizes what I'm doing, straightening her legs and

45

tilting to one side to give me better access. I'm sorry to let her heat out, but this is an emergency.

Ezra still crouches on the floor, looking sour.

"I don't need—"

Bianca huffs. "Get up here, Ezra. I won't freaking bite."

*Unfortunately*, I think I hear Ezra mutter, but her invitation finally gets him moving. He pushes upright, his movements stiff, and kicks his boots off before climbing on the bed beside her. She hisses as he slides under the sleeping bag with her, flinching away from his side before she catches herself and crowds back.

"You're *freezing*. And still soaking wet."

"You're welcome, sweetheart."

Bianca rolls her eyes at his tone, but she can't hide the concern turning down her mouth. She hesitates, then runs a hand over his arm. Starts to rub some warmth back into his limb.

"Maybe… maybe you should take off the wet things?"

Ezra's eyebrows shoot up his forehead. He turns to her, shifting to lay back against the pillow.

"*Bianca*. This is no time for seduction."

"She's right." My own cheeks flush red when he shoots me a wry look. Now she and I match—minus the beard. "The wet clothes will be making things worse."

"Well, well." I can't read his expression as he reaches beneath the blankets, shifting as he peels down his pants. All I know is he won't look away. Ass. "You too, huh?"

*Yes.*

*Always.*

I don't say the words out loud, but they must be written all over my face. Because his eyes widen slightly, and Bianca's staring too. Staring like she's never really seen me before.

Shit. Well. Dignity is a lost cause, I guess.

"Caleb…"

"Just take your pants off, man." I gust out a sigh, then lower to sit with my back to the bed. "God forbid you freeze to death."

# 8

# Ezra

D o I like being stripped and vulnerable, freezing my ass off in front of the woman who just dumped me and the guy she can't help making eyes at?

No. No, I do not.

But do I care once she presses closer, huddling for warmth, her familiar scent washing over me?

Nope. Call me tragic, because this is the best I've felt since she left.

The funny thing is, the way Bianca winds her arms around my waist, pillowing her head on my shoulder—it doesn't *seem* like something she's tired of. More like she needs this just as badly as I do, and neither of us are thinking of the cold.

"I missed this," I murmur into the crown of her head, too quiet for Caleb to hear. Her dark hair tickles my nose.

Bianca says nothing, and for a second it's like she's breaking up with me all over again. My stomach roils, suddenly queasy, and my chest feels way too tight. But then she sighs and inches closer, melting against my side, and her actions speak louder than words.

Thank fucking god.

Suddenly this horrible last month was worth it. Schlepping through this storm was worth it, and not just to make sure she was safe. If there's any chance she still wants this, wants to make things work between us…

I have to try.

Or I'll regret it for the rest of my life.

It's easy enough to pretend Caleb's not here. The cabin is dark, filled with shadows, and he's made of stone where he leans against the bed. His head is turned away, his jaw rock hard beneath his beard, and though he's tensed up, his breaths are slow.

"You smell good."

She huffs a laugh. "I highly doubt that."

"You do, though. Must be pheromones."

She flicks my shoulder, and it's so familiar, it steals my breath. She's flicked me like that a thousand times. Lying in bed together; walking down the street; sipping drinks together in the town bar.

Hope flares to life. Starts somewhere deep in my chest, then spreads outward with every whisper from her. Every time she shuffles closer, plastering against my side. We chat about the last month like we've been busy, that's all. Too busy to catch up, but not estranged. Even Caleb joins in now and then, his low voice soothing.

"Bee," I whisper at last, when I can't take it anymore. It's like nothing has changed between us. "Is this… are we okay?"

She pauses. Then shakes her head in a tiny movement.

*"Why?"* I ask, too baffled to keep my voice down. "Because of him?"

Her silence speaks volumes. Next to the bed, the tips of

Caleb's ears turn pink. And suddenly I want out of this bed, want her arms off me. I start to push upright, kicking the blankets off—

A heavy hand lands on my shin, stilling me.

"Nothing happened." Caleb addresses the opposite wall. He presses down on my leg, pinning me in place. "Nothing ever happened, okay? So stay and get warm."

Oh, I'm warm. The thought of the two of them wanting each other, wishing I was gone this whole time—it's an inferno crackling through me. I'm so warm I'm sweating, fishing around blindly for my wet clothes. I can't believe I let myself hope—made such a fool of myself, *again*—

"Ezra!" Her voice is pleading.

"I'm getting out of here." Where the hell are my fucking pants? My fingers are clumsy as I rummage through the blankets, my bandages from earlier catching against the cloth. "You two can have each other. I won't stand in your way."

"That's not—"

"She doesn't want you gone, you idiot." Caleb turns abruptly, pushing me back down on the mattress with one shove. I let him, taken by surprise. And above me, Bianca shakes her head, eyes damp, her cool hands tugging at me, pulling me back into the cocoon of blankets.

Fine. So she doesn't want me to get hypothermia.

Rational or not, that's not really my concern.

"How long have you two…" I trail off. Maybe I don't want to know. Not with the guilty looks they're darting each other.

"Nothing happened," Caleb repeats. "And nothing ever will, okay? It's an attraction. Nothing more. We never even spoke about it. It can't be helped."

"Like fuck it can't."

Except...

A tiny voice whispers in the back of my head. Calls me a hypocrite. Because it's not like *I'm* some blameless victim here.

How many times have I caught myself staring too long at my best friend? Watching his big hands coiling the climbing ropes, and letting my mind wander where it shouldn't? I always rationalized it away, made excuses for myself—*it's a bodily reaction, a proximity thing, the arousal is a natural response to danger...*

Yeah. I'm no stranger to guilt either.

"This is messed up," I croak, but the fire's gone from my words. Shivers creep back up my limbs, and I let Bianca tug the blankets back over my chest. She tucks me in firmly, like she can pin me down with a pile of blankets and save me from my own reckless decisions.

"I know. Okay? I know. And I'm so sorry, Ezra." She looks so heartbroken, I wish I could make it right for her. Take this all back somehow.

But Caleb's right. It can't be helped.

What a tangle we've gotten ourselves in.

\* \* \*

"Do you remember last summer? The day at the lake?"

An hour later, Bianca's voice is so quiet in my ear, at first I think I dreamed it. But then she exhales softly, shuffling closer, and keeps whispering, her breath tickling my cheek. I strain to listen, my heart pounding louder than the storm, trying to commit everything about this to memory.

The way she feels in my arms.

Her scent.

51

The rasp of her voice, recounting old times the three of us spent together.

It's not like Caleb was always there. Bianca and I spent plenty of time alone, but I can't deny that I know why she brings this memory up.

The days were always sharper, brighter, with Caleb there too. In full technicolor.

"You pushed me into the water." I squeeze her hip, grinning when she huffs a laugh.

"You deserved it."

No doubt about it. "I always do."

"And Caleb pulled you out again."

My grin fades as I remember that exact moment: Caleb reaching over the side of our wobbling row boat, his grip strong and sure on my wrist as he tugged me out of the lake. Water rained down in a shower of droplets, glinting in the sunshine, as he held onto me a split second longer than he needed.

I'd laughed it off. Stripped off my soaking shirt, and pretended I didn't notice the way his gaze lingered on my chest.

Who am I kidding? I'm as guilty in this as they both are.

"Couldn't let the idiot drown." Caleb speaks for the first time in what feels like hours, his deep voice rough. Letting us know he can hear, I guess.

"I *can* swim, you know."

"Could've fooled me. You should've seen him clinging to my shirt on the way up here tonight, Bianca."

It's the easiest thing in the world to swipe out and cuff the back of his head. Caleb chokes a laugh, settling back against the bed, and this time, the silence that stretches between us all is warmer.

Fond.

The comfortable silence of three people who know each other inside out.

"Thank you for coming."

I squeeze her again.

"I'll always come for you."

Caleb hesitates, then adds: "We both will."

The wind moans, rattling the cabin wall. I chew on the inside of my cheek, staring up at the pitch black ceiling. There's something intimate about the darkness. With only the flickering beam of the flashlight to see by, it's like my other senses are heightened. I can hear every breath drawing in and out of Caleb's lungs. Feel Bianca's silky hair sliding over the pillow, a fraction from my skin.

"It was a good day. At the lake." I'm not even sure what I'm admitting. Only that I'm tired of lying to myself. To *them.*

"It was." Bianca scratches a circle on my chest with her fingernail.

Caleb grunts. Guess that's a *yes* from him too.

And maybe my anger is finally fading, or maybe I'm tired, or maybe the storm is getting to me. It doesn't feel *real* out here, in the howling wind and snow, with the wooden boards of the cabin walls creaking around us. We might as well be curled together in the belly of a ship, tossed around on dark ocean waves.

So I shift one leg. Bend a knee, until it's nudged against Caleb's back. Bianca's curled against my side. And fuck it—I want to touch him too. The contact is a patch of warmth, of steadiness, and my racing heart calms a little. Slows down. I've made plenty of excuses to touch Caleb over the years, but now, I don't even bother.

I need the contact. And so does he.

53

And hey—It doesn't count. Not up here, sleepless on Lonely Mountain, in the heart of the storm.

# 9

# Bianca

Caleb freezes when Ezra shifts closer, touching him. Even in the gloom, I can see the lines of his shoulders turn rigid. I hold my breath, too scared to make a sound in case I shatter the spell of this moment.

We've lounged together in a pile before. Watched movies crammed on Ezra's sofa, or sat jammed together on the front bench of Caleb's truck.

But this is different. *Deliberate.* It's like by touching Caleb and I at the same time right now, Ezra has completed an electric circuit. All three of us spark to life.

Breaths grow heavier. The shadows deepen.

Is this… are we…?

For a long while, nothing changes. We all just lie still, touching each other, sharing warmth and breathing as one. But something is changing, nonetheless. Something is breaking and being reforged.

When we begin to move, it feels… inevitable. Like gravity.

Under the blankets, Ezra's fingertips delve through my layers. He moves slowly, giving me time to stop him. To refuse. But

I lay there, heart pulsing in the base of my throat, as he gets closer and closer to my bare skin. And when the callused tips of his fingers brush over my bare hip, my breath catches.

Caleb shifts, the floorboards creaking.

There's the feather-light brush of lips. To my hair... my temple... my cheek. Ezra's not even kissing me, not really—it's more like he's nuzzling me, tracing his lips along my skin. His breaths mist over me, and heat spreads through my limbs.

This is crazy. We're *broken up.* And Caleb is here.

I don't stop him. Ezra's lips trace toward mine.

Distantly, it occurs to me that I'm in no shape to be intimate with someone—not even Ezra, who's seen me after a week of camping before and still ravaged me like a champ. I managed a basic wash after sweating my way through the hike up the mountain yesterday, but I've been soaked by the storm since then, and as my clothes dry against my body, they stink of wood smoke.

But Ezra doesn't seem to care, not as his palm slides boldly over my stomach, and I can't help but crane my neck, offering my mouth up for him to kiss.

The world falls quiet when our lips meet.

We don't speak. What would we even say? The only words that pass between us are soft directions.

"Here." It's so low, I nearly miss it, but then two strong climber's arms bundle me up and over his body. I land with an *oof*, twisted in the blankets, sandwiched on the edge of the mattress between Ezra's chest and Caleb's back.

And what a back it is.

I knew Caleb was a big guy, obviously. You'd have to be blind not to appreciate the sheer *presence* of him, and I have been anything but blind when it comes to Caleb. But seeing and feeling are two different things. Up close, with my palm steadying myself against his spine, I can feel how solid he is: rock hard muscle and heavy bone. His heat scorches my palm through the fabric of his shirt.

His pounding heartbeat vibrates up my arm. He knows what we're doing.

"Caleb," I whisper.

He turns so slowly. Like continental drift. And I half expect Ezra to say something sharp—to get impatient and shatter this moment. But the climber's hands smooth slowly over my skin, never pausing, kneading the curve of my hip. My ass pushes back against him, seeking pressure, even as my hand stays on Caleb as he turns, drawing a steady line over his shoulder blade. His bicep. His chest.

"This is crazy," Caleb rumbles when he's all the way around. At the end of the bed, the flashlight spins to face the far wall, kicked by a stray foot. We're cast in pale shadow—enough light to see each other's features, but still enough darkness to hide. "What are we doing?"

Ezra's shrug rocks me forward. "I don't know."

No. Nor do I.

This is so sudden. It came from nowhere. From a change in the wind, maybe, or the witching hour. Or maybe we've always been two steps from this—hovering on the precipice of crossing this line. Caleb's right—it's crazy, so reckless for us to risk each other like this…

But I won't be the one to stop it, not when I've wanted this so badly for so long. Not when the storm raging outside could bring the cabin down on us at any moment. The non-stop adrenaline of this night has left my teeth on edge, and I want to burn some of these feelings away.

Yeah. That's it.

I want to *burn.*

Ezra's taken us this far, but it seems he's done pushing. He lies pressed up behind me, the proof of his interest digging into my thigh, his hands roaming but not crossing any more lines. My once cold skin is feverish now, desperate for sensation, and my pulse thrums between my thighs

It was never like this with just the two of us. Don't get me wrong—it was *good.* Really good. But it never felt like I'd die if we stopped. I was never crawling out of my own skin with need.

Caleb frowns down at us, holding my hand pressed to his chest, even as indecision wars on his broad, shadowed features.

"Please." I'm not sure what I'm even asking for. Only that if he puts a stop to this, we'll never get this chance again. And it's hard to tell in the darkness, but I think his eyes soften.

"Bianca." He leans forward, pausing an inch from my lips. Glances at Ezra.

Then presses his lips to mine.

I've thought so many times what it would be like to kiss Caleb. So many times, I've lost my train of thought while we were talking—that beard is downright distracting—or laid awake at night, imagining his bulk pressing me against a wall.

I figured he'd be gentle. Tender but careful. The same way he is in every other area of his life.

But Caleb's not gentle. The second his lips touch mine, it's like a change comes over him. A shudder runs through his massive frame, and his hand lands on the bed, screwing up a handful of blankets, as he groans and thrusts his tongue past my lips.

Taking me.

58

*Claiming* me.

Caleb looms closer. He pushes me down into the mattress; he crushes me against his best friend's chest. And I kiss him back with everything that I've got, meeting him with the same pent up desperation.

Who knows how long this will last? I may never get this chance again.

"Jesus," Ezra mutters in my ear, and panic tickles at the back of my mind. God, what are we doing? I don't want to be *cruel.* But Ezra's hands don't leave my skin, and he doesn't roll away on the bed—if anything, he rocks against me slowly, grinding himself against my thigh.

He's into this too. *Really* into it.

I whimper and kiss Caleb harder. It's a battle, all tongues and teeth, and when he nips my bottom lip hard, a bolt of heat shoots to my core.

I want him. I want them both. *Together.*

Right. Freaking. Now.

We're all breathing hard when we break apart—even Ezra, who's only watched so far. I stare up at Caleb, who in turn stares at Ezra. My ex-boyfriend nuzzles my hair.

"This is a bad decision." I need to get it out there. *Someone* should say it, right?

"I love bad decisions," Ezra rasps. "They're my brand."

That's it. That's what we've been waiting for—outright permission, paired with a squeeze of my hip. I bite back a groan, grabbing a fistful of Caleb's shirt and tugging his face down to mine.

I'm not stopping now. Not unless the storm tears the roof off the cabin; not unless a pack of wolves burst through the hole in the wall.

"That's right, Bee," Ezra murmurs in my ear. He brushes my hair over one shoulder. "Show him how good he feels."

# 10

# Caleb

*how him how good he feels.*

Ezra's words land in my skull with a clang, and a war beat begins in my chest. This whole situation is nuts—a scene taken straight from all my shame-tinged dreams—but hearing my best friend say that...

Well. I'd never have conjured that up. It would have shocked me back to reality; shattered the illusion. Reminded me how goddamn tragic my double crush is.

Except he *did* say it, and this *is* reality. And though kissing Bianca is heaven itself, kissing her with him watching, with him urging her on—it's another level. I'm so turned on, my fucking teeth ache.

She's just as bad. Dazed and feverish, unable to keep still as she squirms between us on the mattress. Ezra's arm moves rhythmically, the blankets shifting, and the thought of what he's doing to her under there drags a groan from the depths of my soul. I crowd closer, and now every time he moves his arm, his buried wrist brushes against me too.

I want him closer. Want her wrapped around me, thighs

trembling.

I'm greedy for *everything*.

"Look at you." It takes me a second to realize he's talking to me. When I lift my head, Ezra's eyes are bright, gleaming as they watch me. Laying me bare. "You're starved for her. A man in the desert."

My thumb tracks back and forth across her lip. Back and forth. My eyes follow its movement, committing the feel of her to memory. "Yeah. It's been a long eighteen months."

Ezra sobers then, his forehead creasing, and I wish I hadn't said anything. Why the hell would I mention the way I've been pining after his girlfriend? Talk about murdering the moment. But to his credit, Ezra doesn't nudge me off. His arm doesn't even slow as he works her under the blankets.

A sharp pinch distracts me. Bianca's pearly teeth, digging into my thumb. She lathes the bite with her tongue, soft and soothing, eyes holding mine, then sucks my thumb into her mouth up to the second knuckle.

Ezra drags in a shaky breath, and then he's back with us. Watching her suckle me eagerly, nipping at her earlobe.

"You like being watched, baby?"

She pulls away with a pop. "Only by you."

He likes that. His arm moves faster. And god help me, I can't help speaking up again.

"You can do more than watch."

What exactly am I offering here? I don't even know. All I know is when Ezra shakes his head, the disappointment is a sharp slice between my ribs.

"I have a better idea."

With that, we're bundled upright. Though Ezra is lean, he's corded with hard muscle—strong enough to climb a cliff face with his fingertips. So he moves us easily, a puppet master arranging us on the bed. He sits behind Bianca at the edge of the mattress, his chest to her back and his thighs bracketing her hips. I kneel in front of them, more like an offering at the altar than ever, and Ezra's heel kicks around my thigh. Bringing me closer.

He doesn't stop nudging until I'm pressed flush to Bianca. Until there's no hiding the hard length straining against my pants. The blankets puddle around us, forgotten, and her fingers hitch through my belt loops. Holding me in place, like I might run away. No chance.

With every heaving breath, her chest brushes against mine.

"You wanted each other all this time?" Ezra's voice is ragged. Rough with pain and desire. "Prove it. *Show me.*"

The drumbeat in my chest grows louder.

"What are you..." I can't get my words out. Can't think straight. Not with his heel still digging into my thigh and her big eyes staring up at me, pupils blown wide. "What are you saying?"

Ezra shrugs, the movement deceptively casual. "I want to see. Want to know firsthand what you've both been dreaming about all these months."

"It wasn't like that—" Bianca begins, turning to peer at him, but he takes her chin and turns her back to me. Presses a quick kiss to her cheek.

"It's okay, Bee. I really do want to see."

"No, I mean—"

"We weren't picturing just us two." I blurt it out, saying it so she doesn't have to. Bianca smiles at me, grateful, even as heat floods my face. Screw it. I already let my feelings slip.

For once in his life, Ezra is quiet. His fingers play idly in

Bianca's hair, twirling her dark locks around his knuckles. When he speaks, my heart sinks.

"Call it *my* fantasy, then. The two of you. Together."

So he doesn't want me. Not like that.

It's fine.

Of course it's fine—he doesn't owe me shit, and I'm luckier than any man on earth to have *this* much. A chance to kiss the most beautiful woman alive. But I can't hide the slump of my shoulders, and Bianca's smile is rueful too.

"Your fantasy, huh?"

"Yes." He slides a hand between her legs. "Indulge me. Show me what the two of you would be like."

*Would be.* If this were more than a bad decision made late at night. If this could ever happen again.

A voice is screaming in the back of my head. Telling me to stop now, while there's still a chance to go back. We're breaking something beyond repair, here—tossing nearly two years of friendship into the storm. But his fingers dance over the seam of her leggings, teasing her expertly through the fabric, and Bianca's eyelids droop. She sways in his arms, her grip squeezing tighter on my belt loops.

"Caleb?" Her voice is thick. Like she's struggling to concentrate. Her and me both. "What would you like to do?"

Ah, hell. I can't turn back now. Not when she's eager and willing in my arms, asking what I want next. The answers line up on the tip of my tongue.

*To taste you.*

*Fuck you.*

*Marry you—and live in three-way bliss with your boyfriend. Normal stuff.*

"Whatever you want."

64

"No limits," Ezra murmurs. "My, my. How trusting of you, Caleb."

"Shut up." Even now, he's such a little shit. But it's a relief, really, to hear him ribbing me—it's proof that he's still checked in. Still himself; still bearing an ounce of affection for me.

"I want it all too," Bianca admits in a rush. Her chin turns to the side. "I do, Ezra. Please."

If he's shocked, he hides it well. Ezra hums, thoughtful, then leans to one side and fishes my forgotten backpack off the floor. The first aid kit is jammed at the top, pushed back unceremoniously after I saw to Bianca's side, and he unzips it with steady fingers.

Ezra flicks through it for a split second, then immediately loses patience. Of course he does. The kit goes belly up, shaken out over the tangle of blankets. Band aids and antiseptic wipes rain down in a shower of plastic, but it's the glint of foil that makes my gut clench.

"Suit up." Ezra flicks the condom to me. I catch it, blood pounding. "Let's do this."

# 11

# Bianca

Has there ever been a less romantic statement? Good thing I don't care. Right now, Ezra could speak gibberish and I'd still be into this. As long as his strong chest stayed at my back, his racing heartbeat urging me on.

I can't believe this is really happening.

*Finally.*

Caleb's hands shake as he places the condom carefully on the mattress. He tugs the tail of his belt through the buckle, the thick leather creaking.

This is insane. It can't believe I'm allowed to touch him, after so long of wanting to and holding back. And not just with Ezra's blessing, but with his voice rough with arousal in my ear. He leans over my shoulder, like he wants to get closer to Caleb too.

"You sure about this?"

Caleb nods quickly, jaw flexing, and tugs the top button of his jeans open.

Then he pauses.

He's right. This is awkward as hell. How do you coordinate these things? If it were just the two of us, we'd probably distract each other from the initial fumbling; we'd be caught up in the sensory overload of kissing and rocking our bodies together.

But Ezra's in charge here, not us, directing us with his curt orders and his heated whispers in my ear, and the gap between our bodies feels like half a mile, not a few inches.

There's a dark edge to Ezra's laugh. Shivers race over my skin.

"Suddenly shy, huh? Guess you didn't want each other *that* badly. Don't worry." His spare hand slides down my arm, tangling with the fingers of my right hand. "I'll help get you started."

Caleb has pulled his jeans open, the cloth-covered head of his cock jutting through the fly. And Ezra lifts my hand, guiding us through the void until my fingertips graze against dark cotton.

Caleb's cock jerks.

"So sensitive." Ezra moves quickly, hooking our fingertips in the waistband of the other man's boxers and snapping them against his bare skin. "Come on, Caleb. Be a gentleman. Help the lady out."

Caleb rolls his eyes, but hooks his thumbs in his jeans and pushes them down his hips. After a brief pause, the boxers follow, and the thick length of his cock bobs free in the frosty night air. I want to see all of him, want to shove that shirt off his shoulders and get my hands on that barrel chest too. But there are snowflakes whirling through the holes in our cabin and I don't want to *freeze* the guy.

"Is it how you pictured it?"

I gaze, spellbound, as Ezra guides our hands to Caleb's cock. My hand is sandwiched between them, keeping them separate, but he grips tightly, working us slowly from root to tip and swirling my thumb around the head. My thumb and fingers don't meet, and Caleb's so hot in my hand. So fevered and hard, pulsing under our touch. At the base, there's a thatch of tawny hair, the same shade as his head.

"He's... bigger than I expected."

Ezra chuckles. "Sorry, man."

"No, I—" I break off with a huff. "I figured he'd be big. But that's..."

"A monster?"

I elbow Ezra in the gut, drawing an amused *oof.* "Shut up." Poor Caleb's so red, he looks ready to catch on fire. "You said you'd help, not make it awkward."

"I'm afraid that ship has sailed." Despite Ezra's airy tone, he shifts closer against my ass, his arm flexing as he works us up and down on Caleb's cock. Up and down. His voice drops lower. "Do you like his cock, baby?"

Caleb's gaze pins me too, the question burning in his eyes.

"Yes," I whisper. I mean, come on. I'm only human. And Caleb is what sex toy manufacturers dream of.

"So do I," Ezra murmurs, and that part is just for me. So quiet, I barely catch the words a fraction from my ear. But I do hear them, and heat surges through me in response. *Yes,* this is what I want: the three of us together, equals, all wanting each other—

"Do you want to suck it?"

Hell. Yes.

Caleb makes a small noise as Ezra gathers my hair in his fist, then uses it guide my head down. "Bianca?"

"It's okay." I bend forward, heart pounding. "I like this. He knows I do."

And I guess this *is* easier in some ways, having Ezra here.

68

He already knows what I like and what I don't—knows how to coax my flames higher, then bring me back down before I blaze out too soon. Plus he's taken control, taken the weight of decisions off us both, and my mind is blissfully clear as my lips meet Caleb's cock.

I press a kiss to the tip. Ezra snorts, but I *know* Caleb understands. I know he feels what I'm trying to show him—that sexual frustration isn't the only thing I have pent up for him. There's all this *affection,* too, so much that some nights I felt like I was drowning in it, sucked under by wave after wave of emotions I had no right to feel for my boyfriend's best friend.

"Bianca," Caleb breathes. I brace one palm against his thigh, and feel the muscle trembling.

God. I want him so much.

And so I show him.

"Jesus Christ." Caleb's big hand lands on my head too, petting my hair and tangling with Ezra's fingers. His hips jerk forward an inch, and Ezra hisses in approval.

"Yeah. Be rough with her. You like it, don't you, Bee?"

I hum in agreement, sliding my tongue along the underside of Caleb's cock.

"Everyone thinks she's such a good girl." Ezra discusses me over my head, hand still guiding me, like he's talking about the weather. "But Bianca's a wildcat. She likes it hot and messy; she likes to have bruises in the morning."

"Oh, shit." Caleb's hips jerk harder. Faster. His hand goes from petting my hair to gripping it alongside Ezra's, tight enough to sting my scalp. I whimper, jaw straining, and Ezra tugs me back suddenly, my chest heaving for breath as I sag against him.

"Condom."

Caleb jumps to obey, but then Ezra snatches the packet up anyway. His jaw is clenched tight enough to shatter, and though our eyes meet quickly, neither Caleb or I dare to say a word.

Ezra tears the packet open. Places the condom against Caleb's tip, and rolls it down his cock in one smooth motion, his knuckles squared where he grips the hard length.

Caleb groans between his teeth, and I'm breathing fast too. It's happening. He's touching him, without my hand between them as a barrier. But then Ezra sits back, and he's removed again. The puppet master.

\* \* \*

"Lean back, baby."

Ezra's arms bracket me. He rubs soothing circles over my waist as his friend peels down my leggings and underwear, gaze hungry for every bared inch of skin. I lift my hips to help, and Ezra scoots me forward until I'm hanging off the edge of the mattress. Suspended and helpless between them, held in place by Ezra's arms and Caleb's big hands, lifting and spreading my thighs.

Caleb kneads my thick leg muscles. Stares at my bared sex, expression awed.

"Perfect, isn't she?"

He nods, eyes darting up for a split second.

"Yeah." Caleb gusts out a heavy breath, moving closer. Notching the broad head of his cock against my entrance. "Perfect."

He presses in slowly. So freaking slowly, with Ezra's fingers dancing over my clit. The burn of Caleb's intrusion, mixed with Ezra's feather-light touch—it's a maddening combination.

I whimper, rocking my hips up. Wanting more, *more.*

"How does he feel?" Ezra's breath tickles my ear. "Describe it to me."

"Warm." I squirm, hooking my ankles behind Caleb's back. Urging him an inch deeper with my heels. "Hard. Thick. Like… like he's splitting me open."

"And that's a good thing?" Caleb rasps, his grip tight enough on my thighs to bruise. He screws his eyes shut, thrusting another inch deeper.

"*Yes.*" I'm talking directly to him now, for the first time in a while. "I can feel you *everywhere.*"

"God," Ezra mutters, his composure broken at last, but I don't have time to gloat before Caleb thrusts home. My head tips back automatically, thumping against Ezra's collarbone, and Caleb begins to roll his hips, driving me against his best friend.

I'm caught between them. Held suspended, buffeted against two hard chests, and it's so perfect I could weep. The delicious friction, setting my nerve endings alight; the bruising fingertips; the scrape of teeth on my throat. I lose track of whose hands are where, of who's nipping my ear and rubbing my clit, and they shift me between them, taking turns to hold me up as Caleb's hips keep flexing, pounding away.

It's a maelstrom of sensation, dwarfing even the storm raging outside, and beads of sweat trickle down my spine.

"Does he fuck like you thought?"

"Better," I gasp.

Caleb grunts, fucking me harder. And it's his thumb on my clit now, stroking me steadily, the slower rhythm wringing me out. My heartbeat slams in my ears.

Ezra's palm cracks against my ass. I cry out, hips jerking up, and then I'm coming, muscles shaking, nerves sparking, lights popping before my eyes. They hold me up, Caleb still thrusting, his thumb working my clit to wring out every last whimper—

I slump. Ezra chuckles, holding me up like a rag doll.

One, two more thrusts from Caleb, and then he's swelling inside me. Following me over the edge. His eyes screw shut, a frown creasing his forehead, and both Ezra and I gaze at him, enthralled as that barrel chest heaves.

Brown eyes blink open.

Heavy breaths fill the cabin.

"Well." Ezra breaks the silence after a long pause. "That was new."

It's such an idiotic thing to say, and even Caleb huffs a laugh as he pulls out. I wince, shifting at the new soreness, already so empty without him.

I don't say so. Obviously.

"I hope you don't do that for all your mountain rescues." It's dumb, but at this point I'll say *anything* to break the growing tension. And it works, sort of. Ezra grins, scooting back on the bed and patting the mattress beside him.

"Only the funny ones."

My limbs are clumsy as I stretch out, sweat cooling on my skin. Caleb gathers up the blankets, spreading them out over us, tucking the edges around our tangled limbs.

"We could make room—"

"I'm good." He fastens his buckle, eyes on the floor, then turns and sits again with his back leaned against the bed.

Ezra plays with my hair, and I stare at the man next to us.

No one says anything.

The storm rages outside, buffeting against the cabin walls, and was it this loud the whole time? I almost forgot it was happening.

72

"Goodnight." Ezra leans over, kissing me quickly. That gesture is a balm. Such a relief I could cry.

I glance at Caleb again before answering. "Goodnight."

It was perfect. Better than anything I'd dared dream. But now, lying in the tense silence, I have a sinking feeling that it was a mistake.

# 12

# Ezra

The devastation from the storm is something to behold. We stumble out of Stacey's ruined cabin in the first pale wash of dawn, and after the deafening winds from the night before, the morning is... hushed. Eerie.

The trees stand statue-still, unmoved by any breeze, even with broken limbs hanging by strips of bark. Part of the cabin roof was torn off in the night, tossed against a nearby boulder and folded backward over the rock. All around, there are smashed up branches, lumps of dirt, and other debris, scattered over the sloping mountainside. A layer of snow coats it all, punched through by trails of animal paws.

"Damn." Caleb whistles as he steps out behind me. Bianca presses to my side, blankets wrapped around both of our shoulders. Only Caleb strides out in just his checked flannel shirt—the man is impervious to cold.

"You get through to Beau?"

"Yep." Caleb kicks at a lump of ice. "No major damage in the town. Couple of roads blocked by trees, but that's all."

"That's good." The snow makes me squint as I peer across the slope. After the storm's fury, I thought for sure there would be casualties. "You think your truck's okay?"

Caleb pauses, and then his sigh is the saddest I've ever heard him. He really loves that truck.

"Doesn't matter," he grits out. "We needed to come."

Bianca's small hand shoots out from under her blankets, gripping his fingers tightly in her own. And Caleb looks to me, alarmed, so I force a smile.

"Let's move." I nudge past, throat tight.

It's ridiculous. I mean, they literally screwed in front of me last night—they're hardly crossing a line now. But somehow seeing her hold his hand this morning, in broad daylight, is more of a punch to the gut than seeing their bodies joined in the dead of night.

It's real.

Undeniable.

And it's proof we can't go back.

I know they're not trying to hurt me. I know it's… complicated, between the three of us. But it's first thing in the goddamn morning. I need coffee before I'm going to be a human.

They hold hands for ten minutes. I know, because I watch them out of the corner of my eye, almost tripping over tree roots buried under the snow for my trouble. But the frosty air smells like pine, and it shocks me awake quicker than coffee would, and soon enough I don't even have to fake my grin when I call to them over my shoulder.

"You think the waterfall's frozen? I could ice climb."

Bianca frowns at me, already shaking her head, and Caleb huffs. "If you want to risk that skinny ass, maybe."

I don't. Ice climbing isn't my thing. But their concern warms me from the inside out. And winding these two up is my favorite pastime, so I keep it up as we trail slowly down the mountain.

"You think you two will have a July wedding?"

"Shut up."

*"Ezra."*

"Can I be best man?"

"For fuck's sake." They drop their hands.

We keep it up for forty minutes, the sun inching higher into the pale sky, the crunchy snow glittering underfoot. In the distance, a wolf sends up a mournful howl, and we pause, listening for a reply.

"Must've got separated," Caleb mutters after a minute.

"That's sad," Bianca says. He reaches for her again.

Good. Fine. They're working things out. We're being grown-ups about this, and I am *not* going to wreck the fragile peace between us; not going to risk the two most important relationships in my life. Not even if I want to join that wolf, howling up at the sky. If they want to be together, I need to get the hell over this—or hurt them both. So when I spot another cabin in the distance, I set off with long strides and call out to the man standing outside, gazing up at the roof.

"Hey! You okay?"

The man turns. His arms are crossed over his chest, and his dark hair and pale eyes are almost familiar. A face drifts across my mind—Beau's sarcastic friend from the office. They look cut from the same cloth, with the same aristocratic features.

"We're fine." He has the slight tinge of an accent too. Did they come here together?

"We?"

Another man and woman spill out of the cabin onto the deck.

They're laughing, one with a broom in hand and the other with a camera. Both stop laughing when they see me, falling quiet and moving closer together. The man waves. The woman whispers something.

"Yes." The dark haired man narrows his eyes. "We are good. Thank you."

It's a clear dismissal. So they're fine, not troubled by the storm, but I still don't turn away. Because there's something about the three of them—the way they move together—

The dark haired man rolls his eyes then reaches out. Tucks the woman's hair behind her ear, then kisses the other man, nipping at his lower lip, before turning back to me with an eyebrow raised in challenge.

I wheel around, walking away with my heart thundering. Caleb and Bianca catch up behind me, breathing hard.

"Are they okay?"

"They're fine. They don't need help."

They really don't. All three of them were safe and well, so comfortable together. Surely it can't be that simple?

"Did you ask them if—"

"They're fine, Bee." My tone is short, and Bianca falls quiet again. The tension shimmers between us, put back there by my bad mood.

I sigh, but the damage is done. *For now.* I'll put it right later. My boots crunch through the snow, my hands gripped tightly in my blankets, and as we walk in silence, I run scenarios in my head.

People would talk.

My climbing career could be damaged.

I could lose my sponsors.

All the bitterness and bile the internet has to offer—that

would come my way, without a doubt.

Would it be worth it? Would *we* be worth it? I think of the three people back there, laughing and messing around on that porch. Cleaning up the destruction of the storm with sly laughter and knowing grins.

And as we reach Caleb's truck, half buried in the snow, I pull the stricken man aside.

"Forget about the truck for a second."

"Don't be an ass."

He tugs at my arm, watching Bianca peer through the fogged up windshield. His whole body is turned toward the truck, and his jaw is rigid.

"No, listen." I shake his sleeve. And Caleb finally looks down at me, eyes narrowed. "Let's ask her out. Later today." I pull in a slow breath. "Let's ask her out together."

# 13

# Bianca

I wear a dress maybe twice a year. Three times if someone I know gets married. There's not much call for dresses on Lonely Mountain—especially for the lakeside camp manager. I mean, I wear khaki to work. My best shoes are my hiking boots.

But when your ex-boyfriend and his best friend ask you on a three-way date… it seems like good manners to pull out all the stops.

Stacey sits on the edge of my bathtub as I prop up one foot, dragging the razor along my calf. I'm dressed in sleep shorts and a plain white t-shirt, a towel wrapped around my damp hair, still kind of baffled to find her at my door five minutes ago.

"Bee, I'm so glad you're okay. I'm sorry about the cabin. I'm so, so sorry."

I shoot my coworker a doubtful look. "Why? None of us expected the storm. I took my own risks, Stacey. All you did was offer me a free vacation."

"But—"

"Don't worry about it. Seriously. I'm just sorry we couldn't prevent more damage to your family's cabin."

"We?"

I pause, dragging the razor up my shin. "Um, yeah. Caleb and Ezra came looking for me in the night."

"Both of them?" There's something knowing in Stacey's voice. Her eyes sparkle under the long bangs of her blonde pixie cut. "Is that why you're shaving your legs right after surviving a storm?"

Damn. This isn't normal behavior, is it? But after she came rushing to my door, so worried for me, I kind of feel like I owe Stacey the truth. A sliver of it, anyway. It's not like the whole town won't know in a few hours.

"I... yeah. Yes it is. We're um. They asked me on a date tonight."

Both looking wildly uncomfortable as they asked, but still... it counts.

"And that's what you're wearing?" She wrinkles her freckled nose. I glance down at my rumpled sleep shorts, a purple nail polish stain on their hem.

"No. I figured I'd wear a dress."

Stacey sucks in a sharp breath, and now she looks *way* too excited. She rocks back and forth on the bathtub edge, kicking her heels against the side.

"A dress? Oh my god. You love them. You love them both."

My cheeks heat. "I do not."

"You do, though! You never wear dresses."

"I wore one for New Year."

"Ha!" Stacey crows, triumphant, jabbing a finger at my arm. "Caleb and Ezra were both there, too."

I blow out a long breath, shaving the last strip of my leg and

80

dabbing the skin with a towel. "Circumstantial evidence, your honor."

But we both know I'm full of it.

I love Ezra. I do. I have since the first few months we started dating. But I can't deny that whenever I knew Caleb would be there too... I put in a tiny bit more effort.

The funny thing is, I'm pretty sure Ezra did too. He definitely showed off more when Caleb was there, pushing himself to climb higher or making louder jokes. We were both giddy with the bigger man's presence, vying for the attention of those warm brown eyes.

"You're so lucky," Stacey breathes. "It's like Buy-One-Get-One-Free. Twice the fun."

If only. "More like twice the drama."

She flaps a hand. "Give it time. There are bound to be teething problems. But once you guys figure it out..." She grips my forearm, pinning me with a stern glare. "Tell me *everything*. Every gory detail. Promise?"

I owe her this. Right? For loaning me the cabin. So I nod, even though I'm not nearly so sure anything will come from this. It could be a disaster. An awkward memory we all try to forget—or worse, the final blow which drives us all apart for good. But that doesn't stop me sending up a silent prayer after I've ushered Stacey back through my apartment door.

*Please. If anyone's up there. Please let there be more gory details.*

\* \* \*

The restaurant is *fancy.* The most expensive place in town—the same place my mom took me to celebrate graduating high school. The tables are draped in crisp white cloths and tea lights flicker in frosted glass jars. The center pieces are winter-themed—artfully arranged pine cones and mistletoe wreaths—and soft strains of classical music play behind the murmur of conversation.

Every single person here is dressed to the nines.

I'm really freaking glad I wore my mom's vintage dress. It's pale blue silk, clinging to my hips and waist in a way that makes me tingle.

"You look beautiful," Caleb mutters as the waiter leads us to our table. We draw a few speculative glances from other diners, but nothing crazy. We've hung out plenty of times in public together, after all.

Caleb looks as awkward as I feel, a charcoal suit stretching over his barrel chest. The black shoes poking out from beneath his suit pants are freshly shined, and his beard is neatly trimmed.

"Thank you."

Ezra's head twitches slightly where he's walking in front of us—like he's annoyed Caleb said it first. But when he pulls out my chair at the table, waiting for me to sit so he can nudge it in, he offers a warm smile.

"I'm glad you agreed to this, Bee."

"Me too," Caleb offers.

Another twitch.

I suppress a sigh as I sit, flipping my menu open.

Teething problems. Right? That's what Stacey said to expect. And of course this is weird for Ezra—weirder even than for Caleb and me. He's gone from a loving, long term girlfriend to... this.

A silence so thick, we could spoon it onto our plates.

"So how's the climbing going?" I page through the menu,

trying not to wince at the prices. We're splitting this three ways, right? God, I don't know the rules. "I missed your last few videos."

Ezra has a channel where he posts his best routes and new techniques. It's one of the main ways he gets a following—and sponsors.

"Ah. Yeah?" He shifts in his chair, eyes studiously lowered. "You haven't seen it yet?"

"Seen what?" I drop my menu, suspicion curling through my stomach. All around us, cutlery taps against china. Glasses thump onto the tables.

"He climbed without a rope," Caleb mutters when Ezra doesn't answer.

The floor falls out from under me.

"He did what?" My head whips around. "You did *what?*"

Ezra scowls at his menu, ignoring us both.

"*Ezra.* That's so dangerous. You could have *died.*"

"That's always a risk. Even with a rope. You know that."

"Oh, sure!" I toss up my hands, a bitter smile frozen on my lips. "Then why not hurry it along, right? Why the hell did you do that? Were you punishing me?"

"*No.* It won't happen again, okay? It was a mistake. Drop it, Bianca."

We fall quiet again, both breathing hard, the air taut between us. It's so awkward it's painful, a physical discomfort, and oh god. This is everything I feared. Caleb frowns down at the table, prodding at his soup spoon, but as I'm about to push my chair back and call time of death on this date, he speaks up.

"You know what? I don't know what half these little forks are for."

I exhale, melting back against my chair.

"Combing your beard." Ezra smirks, nudging Caleb's foot under the table, and then we're back again. Mostly normal. Ezra snorts as Caleb plucks up a fork, glancing around before demonstrating, and I muffle a laugh with my hand as a waiter appears, one eyebrow raised.

"Are you ready to order, sir?"

Caleb drops his fork with a clatter, cheeks ruddy. "Uh, yeah. Sure. We're ready."

My turn to nudge him under the table.

For twenty incredible minutes, the date actually goes well. We fall into the same patterns we've always been in, laughing and joking together, but now there's a thrilling edge to every interaction. Promise crackles through the air, making my blood race under my skin, and by turns, we each get caught staring at the other. As the drinks flow and the conversation gets smoother, we lean closer across the table. Ankles tangle and eyes shine.

Then the waiters bring our plates over, lowering first Ezra's and then Caleb's meals to the table.

"Oh, wow." My stomach growls loudly as I stare at their plates. Perfect steak and creamy risotto. "Those look *amazing.*"

Caleb grunts in agreement, and Ezra sends me a wink.

"Maybe I'll let you try mine."

My plate comes last, and the waiter inches around the table to reach me. My back is to the wall, the angle awkward, and I lean back to give the man space.

"Thank you," I murmur as Ezra half stands, Caleb reaching forward.

"I got it—

"Here—"

Three sets of hands collide. The plate wobbles, the waiter

inhaling sharply.

A steaming mound of spaghetti carbonara lands in my lap.

"Ow! Jesus!" I lunge to my feet, my thighs scorched through the thin fabric of my mom's dress. The spaghetti slides onto the floor with a wet slap, my chair screeching over the tiles, and a hush falls over the restaurant as everyone turns to stare.

"Bee." Ezra reaches for me.

Caleb stares, horrified.

"I…" My poor thighs throb under the sticky fabric. "Um, excuse me. I need a minute."

I round that chair, carbonara squelching under my shoes, and muster the last scraps of my dignity as I walk toward the bathroom. Heads turn as I go, whispers picking up, and when I push through the heavy wooden door to the Ladies', my cheeks burn hotter than the food dropped in my lap.

I shove into the nearest stall. Collapse back against the cool wood.

And snort with laughter.

\* \* \*

Half a roll of toilet paper dabbed on my dress later, there's a knock at the bathroom door. If a knock could ever sound apologetic, this is it. I huff out a laugh, tearing off another square of paper.

"Bianca? Are you alright?"

I know Ezra well enough that I can picture his exact expression through the wall. One eye squinted shut, mouth twisted in regret. So handsome, but with such elastic features.

"Yes! I'm good. Just cleaning up." I mop up another splodge of sauce, then toss the paper into the bowl and flush. The bathroom door swings open as I emerge from the stall, and two matching grim expressions watch me from the doorway.

"It's fine. Don't worry about it, guys. It was an accident."

"It's the worst date in existence."

Hard to argue with that. Behind Ezra, Caleb nods in agreement. His cheeks are still ruddy, and even Ezra is flushed with dismay. I cross to the sink, running cool water on my wrists before washing up properly.

"We could order another meal for you?"

"Or run out for a change of clothes?"

I raise a damp palm. "Please, guys. It's fine." And I voice the fear that's been gnawing at me since we first stepped foot in this fancy restaurant. "Maybe... maybe this was a bad idea."

Silence.

Caleb stares at the floor.

Ezra's mouth presses in a line.

My heart kicks against my rib cage.

Crap. Why did I say that? Throw a bomb like that, when it's not a big deal—just some pasta on my dress? I'm sabotaging this, I know I am, but the thought of going back out there with burned thighs and a wet, stained dress...

"We could try again another time?"

They both relax a fraction. But it's still not right. Even Ezra, usually so confident and sharp, is hesitant. I fish for something to say. Anything.

"Um... walk me home?"

The fresh air makes things better. Out in the street, under the blanket of winter stars, with our breath freezing in the air, we can finally laugh about it. Ezra reenacts the pasta falling, his impression of me including his mouth stretched wide in a perfect 'O', and Caleb's laughter booms across the town square.

BIANCA

We fall into step easily with me sandwiched between the two men, and as we walk across town they both move closer.

Ezra's fingers play in my hair.

The back of Caleb's hand brushes against mine.

"Well, you knew we were idiots." Ezra winds my hair around his finger. "Really, this is on you."

"Way to victim blame." My cheeks ache from smiling.

Caleb nudges my other side. "Are you hungry? We could pick you up takeout."

"I'm good." There's a leftover burrito in my fridge with my name on it. "Thank you, though."

Ezra scoffs. "I'm surprised he didn't scrape your spaghetti off the floor for a to-go box. He looked more heartbroken over your lost dinner than you did."

Caleb shrugs, unabashed, and looking up at him, a bubble swells in my chest. He's so good-natured, so gentle and big and kind, and I can't decide what I want to do more: tackle him onto a bed or ride on his shoulders.

"You're drooling," Ezra whispers in my ear.

"Shut up."

Caleb grabs my hand, knotting our fingers together.

The walk home goes by way too fast. And maybe I was hasty, calling this date to an early end. What if this was our only shot? Or what if they carry on the evening without me, then figure out they prefer it just the two of them? What if—

"You're over-thinking." Ezra brings me to a halt outside my apartment's front steps. He smooths away the pucker in my forehead with his thumb. "What's wrong?"

I chew on my lip. "We're going to try this again, right? The three of us?"

Ezra's face softens. Under the streetlights, flecks of gold shine

87

in his green eyes. And when he ducks his head to kiss me, a sense of peace and longing surge through me like a flood.

I've missed this so much.

The way he tilts my head. Cradles my cheeks. Nips at my bottom lip before sliding his tongue past my teeth. Ezra kisses me like he never thought he'd be able to again, and I cling to him, riding the wave.

Something scrapes on the sidewalk behind me. Caleb's boot. Dimly, I remember that Ezra and I aren't alone; that there's someone else we need to consider now. Ezra must realize at the same time too, because he breaks the kiss, his eyes finding Caleb over my head.

"I could leave." The deep voice behind me makes me freeze. *No.* I don't want that—I've *never* wanted that. But Ezra squeezes my hip, knowing, then reaches past me. He backs me up slowly until my shoulder blades meet Caleb's chest.

"Don't bail on us now." My ex-boyfriend raises his chin in challenge. And Caleb blows out a quick breath before settling his big hands on my waist.

"Okay."

He doesn't kiss me. Doesn't take it any further. Caleb stands there and brackets my waist, sheltering me from the cold winter breeze, as Ezra kisses the breath from my lungs. One of Ezra's hands cups my cheek; the other reaches past to hold onto Caleb. Holding his friend in place or steadying himself—I'm not sure.

I'm dizzy by the time he pulls back. Ezra winks before stepping away, and cold air washes over my front.

Caleb lingers a little longer. I think I feel him smell my hair. And then he's gone too, stepping back to watch quietly from the sidewalk.

"So…" I rock on my heels, supremely awkward. "You guys

will call me? Or should I—should we set up a group chat?"

Ezra grins. "We'll figure it out."

"See you tomorrow." Caleb ducks down, dropping a bristly kiss on my cheek before straightening up, face red. He hovers, undecided, then kisses Ezra's cheek quickly too before striding off down the sidewalk, hands shoved in his pockets.

"He's hopeless." Ezra watches him go fondly.

"Yeah. I mean, we all are."

"A good match, then."

One last breath-stealing kiss, and then Ezra's gone too, walking in the opposite direction. If he finds it strange, leaving me here when he's always come inside with me before, he doesn't show it. Even though there's an empty drawer in my bedroom dresser where he kept his things only a month ago. Even though Ezra and I are so much further along together than we are with Caleb.

I hover on the sidewalk, my damp dress freezing to my thighs. Frustration crackles under my skin—this is *not* how I hoped tonight would end. After the frenzy in the cabin, I figured we'd be in a rush again tonight, toppling into bed in a tangle of limbs.

But this is good. Better, maybe. Certainly more mature—even if I'm headed to bed with only my hand for company.

I bite my lip, watching them both disappear around opposite corners. Then hurry back inside, following the siren song of my leftover burrito.

# 14

# Caleb

They don't teach this shit—how to date a couple. How to wedge yourself inside a preexisting relationship without wrecking it. Sure, it's not the kind of thing you learn in school anyway, but with regular two-person relationships, there are books and movies and people all around whose example you can follow.

And maybe half those books and movies aren't like real life, but there's *something* there. A road map.

Here, I'm driving blind.

"Coffee?"

Beau raises his eyebrows at my scowl. I've been glaring at the map on the Mountain Rescue office wall, practically boring two eye-holes through the ancient paper.

With effort, I smooth my brow. "Uh, sure. Thanks Beau."

The older man grunts and squeezes through to our tiny kitchen. Beau is an enigma. He could be thirty five or fifty, I have no freaking idea, and he's so sparing with his words that even though we work together most days, I barely know a thing about him. Just that he lives up on the mountain, and apparently this guy Angelo is crashing with him.

Angelo, who's sprawled over the sofa again, his crutches leaned against the wall.

"You want one?" I call.

Angelo smirks. His features are so *pointy*. "Beau knows what I like."

Sure enough, when the other man comes back, he pushes a mug into my hands before crossing to the sofa. Beau walks with a faint limp, but there's power in his big frame, and when he leans down to hand the coffee over, the two men are thrown into sharp contrast.

Burly and slender.

Ghostly pale and brown skin.

Clean shaven and bearded.

Do Ezra and I look that mismatched? Angelo catches me staring, and a sly smile spreads over his face. "See something you like?"

I turn back to the map on the wall.

We've cleaned up after plenty of storms. This region's known for its rough weather, for its flooding and blizzards and wildfires in the summer, but this most recent one was impressive. Stacey's cabin wasn't the only ruined property, and we were lucky that no one was seriously hurt. But the clean up… it's going to take a while. So I'm several hours in, eyebrow-deep in phone calls and coordinating supply runs, coordinating volunteer clean up crews, when a quiet knock on the door makes me pause.

I shouldn't know her knock off by heart. That's creepy, right?

"Hey, Bianca."

Angelo's eyes are heavy on me as she steps into the office. She's dressed in worn jeans and a puffy jacket, and it's kind of

91

a relief to see her in her normal clothes. She was beautiful in that dress, so pretty I could barely look at her, but this is more *her*. Still beautiful, but softer. Understated.

"Hi." She darts a nervous glance at the other men in the room. Beau ignores her, bent over his cleaning station, his tools spread out ready on his desk, but Angelo cocks his head. She shifts, uneasy. "Um. Do you have a minute?"

Why the fuck is he here? I didn't care until he just made her uncomfortable, but now Beau and I are gonna have words. I push my chair back, fixing Angelo with a hard look.

"Sure. We'll duck into the kitchen."

Angelo's eyes gleam. This fucking guy.

The door snaps shut behind us. It's cramped in here, tiny and battered, with mugs crowding the shelves which line the kitchen walls. I should have offered to go out for a walk, should have taken her for a coffee somewhere, but I'm selfish. I wanted to get her alone.

Bianca doesn't seem to mind. As soon as the door's closed, she smiles shyly and reaches for my hand. Our fingers tangle, and a weight that I hadn't noticed lifts off my chest.

She's not here to end it—whatever this is. I smile back, relieved.

"What is it, honey?" I don't know where *that* came from. I've never called her anything but Bianca. It just slipped out, automatic, but I find I like it. She *is* like honey—sweet and warm and natural.

A pleased flush darkens her cheeks.

"It's Ezra."

Oh. Yeah.

Of course it is. It's ridiculous to think she might have come here for any other reason. They have *history*, so much already between them, and I'm kidding myself to think I'm anything more to them than a plaything. A friend too, yes, but an experiment. A way to rekindle their flames.

"What about him?" My thumb brushes over her knuckles, and I hope she doesn't hear the strain in my voice. God, her hands are small. They felt so freaking good, wrapped around my cock. Soft and feminine.

"I want to do something. For him."

My fingers tingle when I drop her hand, trying to make it seem casual. I scrub my jaw instead, my beard bristling quietly under my palm.

"What kind of something?"

"Um. I'm not sure."

Her weight shifts from foot to foot. There are clumps of melting snow on the toes of her boots.

"Bianca?"

"Yeah?"

"I think you *do* know."

The flush darkens. And yeah, I had it right the first time. She wants to spice things up for Ezra, and I'm her way in. That's fine—it's not like I haven't loved everything we've done together so far—but I can't help the pinch of disappointment in my chest.

What did I expect? Declarations of love?

That Angelo guy had better not be listening.

"He's… he wants you, too."

I clear my throat. "No, he doesn't." Did that sound as gutted as I feel?

"He *does.* I know it."

"Then he needs to say so. I can't assume something like that."

She huffs, frustrated, and I get it, I do. We're all getting tastes of something here, but none of us are getting what we want.

For me, that's the whole damn meal.

"Another date, then. A second attempt. Are you in?"

Now we're talking. I nod, stepping closer, and tuck her hair behind her ear. "I can do that."

"I thought maybe we could climb together."

My laugh bursts out of me, echoing around the small room. "Isn't his ego big enough already?"

"Not in everything." She gazes up at me, so serious. "Not in this."

And yeah, I can see that. Climbing is a good idea—it's Ezra's turf. He's at home there, comfortable in his own skin, built for agility and speed. I'll be a disaster of course, big and lumbering and clumsy, but maybe that's the point. Can't feel threatened by a man like that, can you?

"Thank you, Caleb." She pushes onto her toes, stealing a kiss before I can answer, and I inhale and gather her closer. Crush her to my chest like I'll never let her escape. We stand together, swaying and breathing each other in, and the minutes tick by until Angelo's sharp laughter floats through the closed door.

"I should go." Bianca rocks back on her heels. Her eyes are brighter than before, her pupils blown wide.

I blow out a hard breath. "Okay."

There's a puddle on the tiles when she walks out. Those clumps of snow, melted right off her.

I know how they feel.

* * *

We meet in the climbing gym. The weather's still no good for outdoor climbing—not for Bianca and me, anyway. Maybe Ezra could manage it, but us amateurs would be splattered over

94

the rock. So we settle for the indoor wall, stretching high into the rafters of the gym, but we go after hours. Ezra has had a key for years.

Professional climbers. It's all about who you know, right?

"Interesting choice for a date." Ezra strolls ahead of us, shoulders relaxed. "Very dusty." He glances back at Bianca and winks.

She huffs, but she's smiling too. Pleased at his good mood. And it's contagious, their excitement, especially as we cross the shadowed gym, lit only by sparse pools of electric light. It reminds me of being a teenager, sneaking into places we shouldn't after dark.

"Maybe next time you get up there you should take a cloth."

Ezra snorts. Watching his walk from behind, my eyes snag on his narrow hips in those gray sweatpants. A few inches higher, his muscles flex in his back, the movement visible through his thin black cotton t-shirt.

I rub my palm down my old Mountain Rescue t-shirt, resisting the urge to suck in my stomach. He's a sight, alright.

I spent the afternoon out on the mountain, heading up a clean up crew. Shifting debris; cutting down half-felled trees; in some places, wading through thigh-high water. I'm not a complete slouch, but I've still had alarm bells ringing in my head since Bianca suggested this date. If I wanted Ezra to look at me a certain way... this won't help. I know it.

But I agreed to it—of course I did, she's impossible to deny—and I'm here now. I'll make the best of it. I'll try to enjoy their company, and help them get through this *thing* that they're struggling with.

Honestly, there's a good chance we'll leave here tonight and Bianca's crush on me will be finished too.

"What are you brooding about?" Ezra nudges my side. When did he fall back to walk next to me? We're nearing the wall, our sneakers squeaking over the shiny floorboards.

"I'm not brooding."

"Yes you are."

"I'm…" My arm waves vaguely at the wall. "Planning a route."

"Uh-huh." Ezra pulls me to a halt. His voice drops lower, so it doesn't carry over to Bianca by the wall. She drops her bag on the floor, propping her hands on her hips as she peers up at the handholds. "You don't have to do this, man. Whatever *this* is. She'll be disappointed, sure, but she won't hold it against you."

"And you?"

I can't help blurting it out. I have to know.

"Will I hold it against you?"

"No. Will you be disappointed?"

His mouth firms into a line. I swallow hard, turning back to the wall. "Forget it."

"Caleb—"

His fingers graze my forearm, but Bianca's watching us now too, and this is already humiliating enough. I brush forward, my steps drumming over the floorboards, and force a smile for her.

"Let's just climb."

# 15

# Ezra

There are about a thousand things I'm not sure of right now, but climbing isn't one of them. Coming to this wall, my hands dusted with chalk, and tying the rope through my harness, the movements so automatic I could do them in my sleep... it's a balm. A touchstone in the middle of this chaos.

I smile at Bianca again, so grateful she suggested this as our date, and step up to the route.

*Don't show off,* I tell myself sternly.

Yeah. That lasts about ten seconds.

I can't help myself! Not when I dance up the wall, movements smooth and graceful, and feel my muscles bunch and flex under my skin. Not when I hear Bianca's admiring gasp, or Caleb's rumble of agreement, and push myself to go faster, *higher*. To take a harder route, climbing along an overhang, dangling almost parallel to the ground. To show them that Caleb may be the primordial mountain man, but I have something to offer too.

"You're an ass!" Caleb calls up as I swing myself above

the overhang, his deep voice booming, but it's laced with amusement. I let go of the hold just long enough to flip him off, adrenaline sizzling in my blood.

He yanks on the rope in response, hitching my hips closer to the wall, and damn. That should *not* be kind of hot.

I finish the route with my heart pounding faster than usual. Abseiling down, jumbled thoughts clamor in my head, and when my feet touch down on solid ground, I can't meet Caleb's eye.

"Go on, honey," he says quietly, and I clip out and hand the rope to Bianca. Caleb's tied in to belay: always the protector, always keeping us safe. God, I can't even *look* at him. "Ezra will call up if you get stuck."

Unlikely. Bianca's a gifted climber, always dreaming up creative routes, and she's climbed this wall a hundred times with me before. But she doesn't say any of that—she simply kisses his cheek, ties into the rope, and steps up to the wall.

Shame crowds my throat. Why am I making this all so *difficult?* I snatch up my bag, digging out a water bottle.

It's cool. Refreshing. The distraction I desperately need…

Until I catch Caleb watching the way my throat works. I lower the bottle, scrubbing my arm across my mouth, but he's already turned away. Pulling in rope as Bianca climbs the wall, the back of his neck pink above his shirt.

And suddenly, I'm tired of this. Tired of *myself.* All the dancing around each other, one step forward and two steps back, all the raw nerves and tangled feelings and sharp words. I've been bracing to get hurt since Stacey's cabin. No—since before then. Long before, when I first noticed my girlfriend and my best friend staring at each other, longing etched on their faces.

Since I first noticed him staring at *me*.

"She's good, right?" My voice comes out weird. Strangled and hoarse. But Caleb nods.

"Yeah. Of course she is."

He pulls more rope in, the gear clinking at his waist.

So much faith in her. So much faith in *me*. And though he's proud of her, impressed by her good climbing, the thing is that Caleb would think the sun shone out of Bianca's ass even if she never made it higher than three feet. His regard is a steady thing, warm and solid and dependable, and you'd have to be a fool to drive him away.

*I'd* be a fool.

"Give her some slack. This section is tricky."

Caleb huffs a laugh, but lets out some rope. "You can talk."

We stand shoulder to shoulder, watching Bianca climb above us, and finally, the quiet between us is comfortable. Like it used to be, before everything got so messy, but with something extra there too. The crackle of potential.

"When are you gonna tell her you hate climbing?" I watch him out of the corner of my eye. Caleb grins, his eyes crinkling, and pulls in more rope.

"Not tonight, that's for sure."

"So you're gonna climb?"

"Yeah."

I whistle, long and low. Caleb *can* climb, obviously—it's unavoidable in Mountain Rescue. But there's a world of difference between scrambling over boulders on the mountain and taking on these picky little plastic handholds. He's always hated the climbing gym.

"You must really like her."

He sighs, like I'm dense. "Of course I do. You think I'd put all this on the line if I didn't? I love her, man."

His declaration spreads through my chest like a bruise. I wait, breath held, but he doesn't offer any more. And why would he? I've done nothing but push him away. Why should he take all the risks now?

Caleb clearly agrees, because he stares straight up, jaw hard and eyes focused, belaying Bianca up the route. She skips around the overhang—I don't blame her—but the route she's chosen is hard all the same. Now and then, her soft grunts drift down to us and heat my blood.

"Those little noises," he mutters. "How the hell do you think straight?"

I bark a surprised laugh. "I don't. I never have."

"Explains a lot."

"Shut up."

We're both grinning when Bianca touches back down, her cheeks flushed and her chest heaving from the effort. A light sheen of sweat makes her skin glossy in the dim light, and her fingers shake as she tugs the rope undone.

"Caleb?" She offers him the tail, smile bright. And god help him, he takes it from her without hesitation, passing me the belay line before moving to tie in.

"Wait." My voice echoes through the gym. They both turn to me, expectant. And what the hell am I doing? Caleb's a grown man. He doesn't need a white knight. But knowing he doesn't want to do this, that he just wants to make us happy—it makes my chest so tight, I can barely breathe.

"Wait," I say again. Caleb raises his eyebrows, the rope pinched between his fingers. "I—I want to do something first."

My head buzzes as I knock the rope from his hand. It swings back, thumping softly against a hold, and Bianca's gasp cuts through the quiet as I push Caleb back against the wall. He goes easily, eyes wide, and I grab a fistful of his t-shirt, squeezing the fabric as I lean forward to kiss him.

His groan vibrates down to my bones.

Caleb's mouth opens, our tongues sliding together, and we're pressed closer than we've ever been. I've wondered how this would be for so long—pictured it almost non stop since the night in the cabin—but I could never have conjured the warmth radiating off his body, the wood smoke and pine scent of him, how *hard* he is under those baggy shirts. Not the sculpted hardness of a climber, but the solidity of a man carved from the mountains. I could climb Caleb like a damn rock face.

Sharp teeth nip my lip, and I grunt and push closer. I want *all* of him; I want everything Bianca got and more.

I want him together and separate, morning and night, and why the fuck have I been resisting this?

"Wow," Bianca whispers behind me, and I reach out blindly, scrabbling for her hand. She snatches mine up, knotting our fingers together, and lets me pull her close. I want them surrounding me, want them *both*.

We break apart, breathing hard. Caleb's still staring at me, eyes wide, and I thump my fist against his chest.

"I love you," I rasp at him. Bianca squeezes my hand, urging me on. "I've been an idiot about this, but it's still true. And I don't care if you're not there yet. Don't care how long it takes. I'm going to make you love me too."

It's a shit declaration. But when I drop to my knees, Caleb's hand goes straight to my head, fingers carding through my hair. I tug his sweatpants down and he chokes out a cough, so I force my gaze to his.

"Yes?"

He darts a glance at Bianca behind me. Whatever he sees, his forehead smooths. And then he nods, throat bobbing, his grip tightening in my hair.

"Yes. Fuck yes."

# 16

# Bianca

I've always felt like kind of a pervert for picturing my boyfriend with another man. Not just picturing it—getting off on it. Finding the thought so freaking hot, I couldn't help but touch myself.

Right now, watching Ezra take Caleb's cock in his hand, I am vindicated.

See? I'm not perverted.

I'm a goddamn visionary.

Caleb looks startled, his eyes as wide as the first time we reached for him in Stacey's cabin. But his fingers play idly in Ezra's dark hair, and when the other man drags his fist along his cock, Caleb's groan sends a pulse of heat to my core.

I inch closer, not daring to speak.

I don't want to break this spell.

God knows what the pair of them said to each other when I was up that wall, but whatever it was, I'm glad. Ezra's still gripping my hand like a lifeline, his other hand working Caleb's cock, and when he glances at me with a question in his eyes, I stroke his hair too. His eyes dip closed, his head butting into my palm like a cat, and *yes.*

Of course I want this for him. For both of them. For *us.*

I nudge him towards Caleb's cock.

Ezra doesn't tiptoe. He doesn't do things by halves. So when he opens his mouth, his tongue darting out to wet his lip, Caleb and I both watch with our breath held. And sure enough, Ezra takes him deep straight away, sucking so hard his cheeks hollow.

His dark head bobs.

The soft sounds fill the climbing gym.

"Shit. *Shit.*" Caleb's head slams back against the wall. His free hand scrabbles along the surface, latching on to a climbing hold, and his fingertips are white where he clutches the plastic. His hips jerk forward, his face pained.

Ezra hums, taking him deeper.

"Show off." I nudge my boyfriend with my toe.

He is my boyfriend, right? That's what this means. We're back on—all three of us. The last cold, lonely month was a nightmare, but now we're waking up. Giving in to the unstoppable pull between us.

Ezra's hand tugs me down, and I drop to the floor automatically, the thump echoing up to the rafters. Faint pain hums through my kneecaps, but I don't care. Not when he shuffles over, making room for me between Caleb's feet, head still bobbing.

"This is not a standard couple's activity," I whisper, kneeling closer. Lifting our joined hands to grip the base of Caleb's cock.

Ezra lifts his head, his voice louder. Certain. "We're not a couple."

Panic. Bright, ringing panic.

"But—"

He snorts, nudging me with his shoulder. "Come on, Bee.

You can count."

Relief and joy spread through me, warming the hidden nooks inside my chest, and when I look up at Caleb, I find the same happy glow reflected back. He stares down at us, eyes flicking between Ezra's lowered head and my hand on him, and I lean forward. Press a kiss against his sweatpants-clad thigh.

Ezra pulls off again with a wet pop, swirling his tongue around Caleb's head. I watch, one eye narrowed as our hands pump at the base.

"How are you so good at that? Have you done this before?"

Ezra rolls his eyes, not stopping. Above us, Caleb chokes out a laugh. Then: "It's not rocket science, Bee. I do have one of these."

Oh, yeah. It's a timely reminder. I reach for Ezra's waistband, grinning when his breath catches. He shifts his hips from side to side, helping me to ease his sweatpants and boxers down, and he watches me with heavy-lidded eyes as I pull his cock out too.

So far, it's been all me. All Caleb. And Ezra's watched, he's been involved and in control, he's absolved us with his blessing, but he hasn't got off. Not once.

He's supported us, even when it hurt him.

And now, it's his turn to feel good.

Caleb clearly agrees, because he eases Ezra off his cock, tucking his painfully hard length away before circling behind me. His steps thud against the floorboards. He taps once on my shoulder, and it's so easy, moving together. Like it's a dance we've all learned, rehearsing in our separate shame-tinged daydreams ready for this moment.

Ezra stretches out on his back. I shove my leggings down quickly and straddle his hips. Behind me, Caleb rummages in Ezra's backpack, then kneels over the climber's legs. We rearrange in the space of a few breaths, breaking apart then snapping back together, three magnets clustered together in the pool of electric light.

Caleb's arms wind around me, bracketing me with his big muscles and his scent. I tip my head back and kiss his neck.

"Stop distracting him." Ezra pinches my hip. I turn back, poking my tongue out at him while Caleb slides the condom onto our boyfriend.

"Go on, honey." Caleb urges me up, hands gripping my hips. He tugs my underwear to the side, then guides me over Ezra's cock. "Take him. Show me how you take him."

*Like this.*

With my cheeks flushed and my lips parted. Breaths ragged as I ease myself down. For all Ezra's joking about Caleb's cock, he's big too—big enough to stretch me, to make me work for it—and he runs soothing palms up and down my thighs. Caleb is *everywhere*, looming over me, his heat at my back and his scent in my lungs, and he's merciless in the way he lifts my hips up. Holds me poised, teetering on the edge. Then slams me down, wedging Ezra home.

The breath empties from my lungs.

"*Fuck.*" Ezra stares up at the ceiling, glassy eyed. He's going to leave fingerprint bruises on my thighs.

"How does he feel?"

"Good." It's a croak. "S-so freaking good."

"I bet." My head tips back, lolling on Caleb's shoulder as he keeps lifting me. Slamming me down. His words are hot against my ear, his beard tickling my neck. "You know how many times I've pictured this? You and him. I fucking knew it would be like this. Fucking magic. Like a goddamn wet dream."

"Not just him and me. You're here too."

Jeez, I can't think straight. Not with the thick slide of Ezra inside me, and all these bruising, gripping hands, so freaking perfect as they guide me where they want. Passing me between them, like in the cabin. There's no storm tonight, no easy excuse for what we're doing. This doesn't feel *unreal*.

It's us. We're doing this. Our rough breaths fill the climbing gym; our shadows move together on the wall.

"Yeah. Yeah, I am." Caleb nips my earlobe, sharp and sudden, and I cry out, pitching forward and bracing my hands on Ezra's chest.

A heavy palm slides up and down my spine. Up and down. And I take over the rhythm, my hips rolling as I fuck Ezra into the ground.

It's not enough. I mean—god, it *is* enough, I'm barely holding back from coming as it is. But I want more. The three of us, tangled so tightly together that it would be impossible to undo.

Ezra knows what I want. He always knows.

"'S lube in the bag," he grits out. "And another condom. Be careful with her."

"You brought lube to the gym?"

Ezra smirks at me, reaching up to twirl an escaped strand of my hair.

"What can I say? I'm a romantic."

The crack of a bottle lid makes my heart skip. Caleb rubs a hand up my back, nudging my t-shirt out of the way. He pauses at my underwear, pulled to the side, then quickly tears it off at the seams.

Holy shit. Who knew? But I don't even have time to process that, because something slick and warm drips down the center of my ass.

107

Oh god. I've never done this. I've never been touched *there,* not even when Ezra asked once, and the rueful smile he gives me tells me he's thinking of that too. Something brushes against the line of my ass—a fingertip. And shame floods me automatically, hot and overwhelming.

But Caleb's touch is gentle, so steady and reassuring. Just tracing up and down, not delving any deeper.

And Ezra's eyes on me are so tender. Filled with so much love, it makes me ache.

"Relax, baby. We can stop any time you want. Okay?"

I nod, teeth chattering. And ask, "Caleb? H-have you done this before? At the same time as another man?"

There's a heavy pause. Below me, Ezra's eyes widen with wicked delight.

Then: "Uh. Yeah. Yeah, I have."

"Fuck me." Ezra strokes up and down my thighs. "It's always the quiet ones."

"Shut up." I flick his chest, then turn back to Caleb. "I'm glad. It's a relief, actually."

His kiss slows my racing heart. It chases away all that shame. "I wouldn't have hurt you either way."

At some point in the last few minutes, my hips stopped moving. Ezra's still lodged deep inside me, still so hard I can feel him throb, but as Caleb's fingertip circles closer and closer to the pucker of my ass, there's no sense of hurry. I'm gathered against one sculpted chest, kissed and whispered to and soothed, while another looms at my back and eases the first knuckle in.

It's so *much.* So intense I can't tell if it's good or not. I suck in a sharp breath, and Ezra snakes a hand between us. As he rubs my clit, Caleb's finger slides deeper.

And… okay.

I rock my hips back a fraction. I think I get it.

It's so alien, so unlike anything else, but the overload of sensation—it heightens everything else too. And as I get used to it, as Caleb gradually adds another finger, I go from unsure to so desperate I could cry.

"Please." Complete sentences are beyond me. I rock back against Caleb's hand, urging him deeper, feeling Ezra everywhere inside me. *"Please.* Now. Do it now."

It doesn't matter that we're all sweaty. That we're in an empty climbing gym, with the wind moaning outside the high windows and a pool of light flickering at the other end of the room. All that matters is that we're together, gripping each other tight, driving each other higher and higher, our ragged breaths in sync.

When Caleb presses inside me, the burn is almost too much to bear.

*Almost.* But then he's in, and I practically float up to the ceiling.

Forget climbing. This is flying. This is riding the ultimate storm. We move together, clumsily at first, but once we find our rhythm, it's unstoppable. Caleb's grunts mingle with Ezra's groans, and I soak up every sound. I lick Caleb's throat; I scratch Ezra's chest through his t-shirt.

"Bianca." Dazedly, I blink down at Ezra. His expression is awed. "Baby. I can feel him. *Fuck.*"

I break first. I wish I could drag it out longer, wish I could live suspended in this moment somehow, but I can't. Not with Ezra's thumb on my clit and both of them moving inside me. My orgasm rolls through me like thunder, slow at first, coming from a distance, then so powerful it shakes my foundations. I cry out, my voice bouncing up to the rafters.

Caleb's grip tightens on my hips. He drives deep, swells bigger, and empties inside me with a groan.

Ezra comes last, with his eyes screwed shut.

We cling together for a long pause. Then peel apart, sticky and wincing. My legs are wobbly as I tip onto the floorboards, my breaths still loud.

"Sorry about your underwear." Caleb picks up the ruined scraps of cotton, mouth twisted. He flips it over in his palm. "I'll buy you new ones."

Ezra splutters. Then drops his head back and *laughs*, a big, booming laugh that fills the climbing gym.

"I really don't think she minded, man."

He's right about that.

# 17

# Caleb

They come back to my place. I don't know why I'm surprised—it's not like they haven't made themselves clear. Bianca and Ezra both want this. They both want *me.*

But my cabin's a mile out of town. I figured they'd be done with the wilderness for a while. Figured they might want some time alone together. To talk; to figure out our new dynamic away from my ears.

Apparently not.

"Could you be more of a cliche?" Ezra strolls around the open plan cabin, hands shoved in his pockets as he leans down to peer at my bookcase. "*The Call of the Wild*? Come on, man."

"You've been here hundreds of times. You're only just noticing?"

Ezra glances over his shoulder, mouth curled in a smirk. "Guess I'm seeing you through new eyes."

*New eyes.* That's one way to put it, when your best friend declares his love, drops to his knees, then shares his longtime girlfriend on a climbing gym floor. Two hours and one very

111

crowded shower later, I still can't believe it happened. That they're really here.

Bianca calls out from the kitchen. "Anyone want coffee?"

I mean, it's so freaking domestic. And I don't do this—don't have people here like this. Getting settled. Claiming armchairs and hanging their jackets on the back of the door. Ezra already prowled right into my bedroom, flipping back a corner of the bed covers like he was folding down the page in a book, saving his place for later.

"Uh, yeah. Sure. Thanks, honey."

*Honey.* Seriously, who the hell am I right now? My cheeks are so constantly flushed tonight, they might stain permanent red.

"Give him two sugars," Ezra yells. "He's freaking out again."

"I am not—"

"Caleb? Are you okay?" Bianca's head pokes around the kitchen door frame, her eyebrows pinched with concern. I toss my hands up, so goddamn flustered.

"Your boyfriend's being a prick. I'm fine."

She hums. Clearly doesn't believe me. But she shrugs one shoulder and disappears back into the kitchen. *"Our* boyfriend now, Caleb."

That echoing call is the last straw. A headache begins pounding in my temples, gripping and squeezing my skull. I scrub my eyes, stifling a groan. And behind me, Ezra clicks his tongue.

"Yeah, I know what this is. Buyer's remorse." His voice drops, so Bianca can't hear. "Are you having second thoughts?"

Yes. No. Not—not about *them.* I've known how I feel about them both for far too long.

But I've barely dated one person at a time. And this is so much more complicated, more important than any relationship I've had before, and if I fuck it up, I lose them both.

God. I'm definitely going to fuck it up.

"I just... I..."

Suddenly Ezra's right in front of me, hands on my shoulders. His face is more serious than I've ever seen it before. The fire pops in the grate behind me, heat licking at the backs of my legs, but it's nothing to the emotion burning in Ezra's eyes.

"You need to say if you regret it. You can't lead her on. I won't let you. She loves you too much."

And there it is: what brought us here. What soothes the fierce ache in my skull.

She loves me. So does Ezra. And I sure as hell love them both.

"Sorry," I mutter. "I don't regret it. This is what I want. It's just... new territory for me, that's all."

"That's not what you said in the gym." He smirks, eyes dancing. "We're going to need those details later."

"No!" I bat at his chest. I guess I can do that now. "God. That's so weird."

"What's so weird?"

"Nothing," I say quickly. Bianca winds between the scattered armchairs, three steaming mugs gripped in her hands. I got a third armchair here the week after I met her. I wasn't even thinking about it really, I just figured Ezra might bring her round sometimes and I wanted her to feel at home.

Maybe I should get a big corner sofa now. So we can lie there together. Or one of those playboy mansion massive beds.

"He's going red again."

Ezra chuckles. "He's fine."

"How do people do this shit? Three-way living." I take the offered mug, nodding at Bianca. And once I've started looking

113

at her, I can't stop. She's lit by the golden glow of the fire, so goddamn beautiful with a peaceful smile on her face.

I don't think I've ever seen her this happy. She's always seemed kind of strained.

Guess I know why now. Guess we *all* know why.

"Is it that different?" She blows on her coffee, lips pursed. "If anything, it'll be easier. I've been dealing with this idiot on my own. Now there's two of us to walk Ezra."

He snorts. He loves it when she gives him a hard time.

We cluster around the fireplace, shoulder to shoulder, sipping from our mugs. Warmth everywhere, with the wind moaning outside the cabin.

Yeah. She's right. It's not that different—not where it counts.

And we've been building up to this for a long, long time.

# 18

# Bianca

*hree months later*

T It's the first cookout of the season. The weather's probably too cold if we're honest with ourselves—there are no flip flops or t-shirts on display. A cool breeze ripples the water at the lakeside, and the sunlight is pale and weak.

Doesn't matter. The locals have braved another winter on Lonely Mountain, and we're going to celebrate, goddamn it. Everyone's here, dropping coins into the Mountain Rescue collection buckets, grabbing up frosted beer bottles and lining up for hot dogs off the grill. Beau stands guard, tongs in hand, flipping the cooking meat with loud sizzles and nodding silently as he receives each new order.

"Hot dog or burger?" Caleb comes to stand at my back, kneading my sore shoulders. I cleared out the lakeside cabins yesterday with Stacey, getting ready for the summer camp season, and I've been paying the price all morning.

I moan, tipping my head back, his question already forgotten. Damn, he's good at that.

"Hey, you two. This is a family friendly event." Ezra shoulders through the crowd in front of us, three beer bottles in his hands. He passes us one each then swigs from his own, and I watch the column of his throat bob, mouth suddenly dry.

Right. Right.

Family friendly event.

Clearing my throat, I tear my eyes away and scan the crowd. Stacey waves from where she's perched on a picnic bench, chatting to the guy who runs the town pharmacy. She eyes my dress pointedly, the thick red cotton blowing against my thighs, and gives me a wink.

I hide my smile with a swig from my bottle.

Beau's at the grill, which means—*there*. A little ways behind, leaning against the brick wall of the camp reception building, Angelo stands apart from the crowd. Watching Beau. Always watching. He used to freak me out so badly when I first started visiting Caleb at the Mountain Rescue headquarters, but now, I can look at him without shivers running down my spine.

That longing etched on his face—it's pretty damn familiar.

I don't know what the hell's going on with those two, but whatever it is... it's intense.

A burst of laughter sounds above the crowd. The sound is infectious, so joyful, that as I turn to look, my face cracks automatically into a smile. Three people are coming to join the cookout, strolling side by side along the lake's edge. They chat as they walk, a taller, fair-haired man nudging a curvy woman with his elbow. All three are vaguely familiar—faces I've seen in the town stores, or nodded at politely on the hiking trails. People who I'd assumed were tourists, but who apparently live here year round.

One of them—a pale man with dark hair—looks a lot like

Angelo. Frowning, I turn back to the grill just in time to see Beau's friend slip away, ducking neatly around the corner of the building.

Huh.

Caleb's beard tickles my ear. His breath is warm as he murmurs, "Those three by the lake look pretty close."

"Infidels," Ezra agrees loudly. "Flaunting their three-way love. Who would do such a thing?"

There are a few splutters of laughter. Some whispers, too. Out of all of us, Ezra's gotten the most heat for our relationship. He even lost a few sponsors and big trips at the beginning. He insists he doesn't care, that people are small minded and that's not his problem, but I know it hurt him. So he makes a point to kiss us both in public. To hold our hands, eyebrows raised at anyone who dares to make a comment.

It's a little more drama than I'd choose for myself, but for Ezra... sure. I'll take a stand.

"Here." I grab the climber's belt loop, tugging him close. "Let's give them something to gossip about."

The moment his lips touch mine, cooled by the beer, my heart slams harder in my chest. This feeling never seems to fade. Not with him; not with *either* of them. Ezra smirks, his mouth curving against mine, then tilts my head. Deepens the kiss.

"Family friendly..." Caleb mutters in the background.

The newcomers glance at us, openly curious, as they make their way to the grill. The woman ducks into the crowd, returning to her partners with three bottles. They murmur greetings to a few people, but to most, they seem to be strangers.

Beau serves the dark-haired man a burger. Then does a double-take, eyes wide.

117

"I think our time as the hot town gossip is over," Ezra says sadly. We watch together as Beau leans forward, muttering something in the newcomer's ear. The man stiffens, pushes the burger back into Beau's hand, then shoves through the crowd and stalks back toward the lake. The other man and woman follow, hurrying to whisper together. He shakes his head, agitated, and the three step off the path, ducking into the trees.

"Very dramatic." Caleb twirls a lock of my hair around his knuckle. It's a habit he picked up from Ezra. "Place your bets, people."

"Witness protection."

"A secret half brother."

"An evil clone."

"Bianca," Ezra says flatly. "Clones are identical. Get your head in the game."

I grin. "Fuck off, Ezra."

"Family friendly," Caleb reminds us, voice strained.

Okay. Yeah. We're not quite public-ready. Especially not after three months holed up in Caleb's cabin, barely coming up for air. After spending the spring wrapped up in each other, learning new ways to be together, we might have gone a tiny bit feral.

I lean my head back against Caleb's chest. Feel the breeze on my cheeks as Ezra sidles closer, hooking his finger around mine.

We'll figure it out. And the town will get used to us.

Because the three of us—we're not going anywhere.

* * *

118

Thanks for reading Her Mountain Rescue! If you want more mountain menage, I've got you covered.

Because Angelo finally gets his story in Their Mountain Bride! >:)

# Teaser: Their Mountain Bride

Well, I did it. I humiliated myself in front of the whole town—with Beau Walker's help of course. I ruined twenty-five gossip-free years in one night, and made myself a laughing stock.

They'll get over it. There are plenty of weirdos on Lonely Mountain to cause a scene, and I'll be old news in a couple of weeks. I know that, and yet I still flush bright scarlet when Beau Walker squeezes through the library entrance and two dozen heads spin to me.

No.

*Look away, you assholes*, I beg them all in my head, crouching ridiculously low and scuttling along an aisle. My shelving cart is left abandoned, blocking the stack, but it's too late to turn back. I need to get out of here, right. Freaking. Now.

I'm an idiot, okay? I got caught up in all those cheesy movies I binge in the evenings after work, and I saw the books Beau Walker checked out on his record, and I figured I knew him somehow. That we were sappy kindred spirits, die hard romantics in a cynical world, never mind his constant scowl.

But he put me right. I know better now.

And I don't want to wave awkwardly as he browses the stacks. I don't want anything from Beau Walker. Not anymore.

"That room's reserved," one of the elderly ladies at the knitting tables calls over. I roll my eyes, turning the handle to one of the private reading rooms nice and slowly, so it doesn't squeak. Pulling it open a crack, I find it blissfully empty.

Aha!

Suck it, Audrey.

This will do nicely. I slip through the opening, closing the door softly behind me, and flick on a desk lamp nearby.

The reading rooms are a throwback, designed for privacy and serious study, but you don't get a lot of either in this town. A sturdy desk rests against one wall, an empty shelf on the wall above, and two spindly chairs take up most of the floor. The window is big, stretching right across the far wall, and the glass panes are still fogged from the morning chill.

The sun hasn't reached this side of the library yet. It's cold in here, and I hug my waist against a sudden shiver.

The door opens before I can react. A pale, dark-haired man slips through, moving on silent feet, and closes it with a muffled click before turning to face me.

"You're Beau Walker's friend."

I know this guy. He's been living in Beau's cabin since last fall. He was the favorite topic of town gossip for months—at first, because of his dramatic accident in the river, and once he was healed, because he freaked people out.

His eyes, they said. They're bottomless. Dead and predatory, like a snake.

The man crowding into the reading room with me, though—he's not dead-eyed. He's smirking, mischief sparking in his fine-boned face.

"Um, can I help you?"

I don't know what else to say. *Fuck off* is not in my DNA.

The man takes me in, his roving gaze leisurely as it slides down my front, all the way down to my ankle boots, then back up my jeans and pink t-shirt.

He smiles wider.

"Hello, Katy Poole. You're hiding from Beau."

I splutter. I am, but it seems rude to point it out. "And you are?"

"Angelo."

"Angelo who?"

"Angelo Smith."

Yeah, right. This guy's last name is no more Smith than mine is. But he stares at me, challenging me to call out the obvious lie, and I falter.

Crap. I'm no good at conflict.

"What do you want, Angelo?" I read once that to defuse a tense situation, you should repeat a person's name.

"I saw the books."

Perfect. Well, who hasn't at this point? Gossip travels like wildfire through this ridiculous town.

"And I read your note."

That gives me pause. Because as far as I knew, no one else had found out about that. It was the one thing I had to thank Beau Walker for—that he didn't spread it around the whole damn town that I asked him out to dinner. Right before he reamed me out for trespassing at his home.

So, okay. This guy Angelo knows. Which means what he does with that knowledge is officially beyond my control. I try very hard not to get hung up on things I can't influence.

Even things with sharp cheekbones and knowing smiles. Even extremely handsome things.

See, this is the problem with a non-stop diet of romance novels and cheesy movies. You start projecting those story lines, seeing meet-cutes and swoon-worthy figures in real life, when in reality, they're just… a disappointment.

And I'm done with that. Beau Walker has officially shamed it out of me. So I draw myself up to my full, tiny height, and pin Beau's friend with a frosty glare.

"That doesn't matter now."

"No?"

Angelo leans against the wall beside the door, his arms folded over his chest. I try not to notice the way his muscles bulge beneath his sleeves.

"No."

"Why not?"

"Because Beau wasn't interested. And he was an asshole."

That smirk grows wider. And damn me, there's something magnetic about this guy. I feel the corners of my mouth tugging, trying instinctively to smile back. My heart lifts, the tightness in my chest easing, even though there's no good reason for me to find this guy reassuring.

"*I* liked your note."

I fiddle with my lanyard. My cheeks are warm. "Um. Thank you?"

"Do you know why Beau is here?"

My shrug is clumsy. Like I've forgotten how bodies work. So my quiz master takes pity and answers for me.

"He's having second thoughts. He thinks he may have been hasty." Angelo pushes off the wall, his arms dropping to his sides, and for a crazy moment my breath catches in my throat. I've never been trapped like this in a small space with a strange man. I thought it would be nightmare fuel, not make me all tickly and restless, a vivid slide show of what we could do in here flickering in my mind's eye. "Do *you* think he was hasty?"

"I don't…" My brain won't work. Especially when Angelo

123

reaches out, tucking a stray lock of hair behind my ear. His fingertips linger, tracing a soft line over my cheek. "I don't know."

His hum is soft. Low. I bite down on my lip. And when he steps back, I exhale in relief, sagging on my feet.

"Beau is no good for you." The change in his tone is abrupt. From warm to warning. "Better to keep your distance."

Um, what? I stiffen, the flutters in my belly dying away in a blink. I know that, I don't need some stranger weighing in. Warning me off like a jealous boyfriend. The reality of my situation floods back in: I'm hiding at work, tucked away in a small room with a stranger who touched my *hair*.

"Excuse me." I scrabble for the door handle, yanking it open regardless of the noise. If Beau Walker sees me after all, so be it. I'm done with this conversation. "I should get back to work."

Angelo doesn't move as I plunge back out into the stacks, cheeks flushed. And when he speaks, it's so quiet, I barely catch it at all.

"Good to meet you, Katy Poole."

I snatch my shelving cart and set off, the wheels bumping over the carpet.

# About the Author

Kayla Wren is a British author who writes romance with heat and heart. She loves Reverse Harem, Enemies-to-Lovers, and Forbidden Love tropes.

Kayla writes prickly men with hearts of gold, secretly-sexy geeks, and—best of all—she's ALWAYS had a thing for the villains.

**You can connect with me on:**

🌐 https://www.kaylawrenauthor.com

🔗 https://www.bookbub.com/authors/kayla-wren

🔗 https://www.amazon.com/~/e/B08CL281V1

**Subscribe to my newsletter:**

✉ https://www.kaylawrenauthor.com/newsletter

# Also by Kayla Wren

**Year of the Harem Collection:**
Lords of Summer
Autumn Tricksters
Knights of Winter
Spring Kings

**Standalone titles:**
The Naughty List
Roomies

**The Office Hours trilogy:**
Extra Credit
Bonus Study
After Class